Richmond S. Dement

Napoleon

A drama

Richmond S. Dement

Napoleon
A drama

ISBN/EAN: 9783337350611

Printed in Europe, USA, Canada, Australia, Japan

Cover: Foto ©Andreas Hilbeck / pixelio.de

More available books at **www.hansebooks.com**

LIEUTENANT BONAPARTE.

A DRAMA

—BY—

RICHMOND SHEFFIELD DEMENT

READING EDITION

WITH APPENDIX

CHICAGO
KNIGHT, LEONARD & CO.
1893

Ah! Ah! Ah! Poor Josephine! Alas! Alas!
She gave her life a willing sacrifice;
And I, with my own hands, tore out her heart
And mine, and laid them bleeding on the shrine
Of France!
But to what end? That the hell-hounds of Fate,
The damned hag, should lick the flames up
From that altar's crest, to follow hot
Upon my track forever after!

                         (*Napoleon*, *Act VI, Scene Second.*)

PREFACE.

TO LOOK upon a great landscape is to be wrapped in a glorified enthusiasm. The grander the scene, the more magnificent, the easier its possible reproduction appears to the artist. This is his instant thought. It is born of his delight. When he comes to his canvas he realizes that enthusiasm is not inspiration.

The limits of the stage are scarcely less circumscribed than the canvas and, may I urge, the demands of the sublimest of earth's pictures are not more inexorable than the career of Napoleon. This immensity has been at once the spur and the discouragement and I can but trust the present work will be more satisfactory to others than it is to myself.

I have, perhaps, not presented the popular Napoleon. I have endeavored to portray Napoleon as I am convinced he will appear in a not far distant period of unfettered truth.

The facts upon which I have based my work have been obtained through careful comparisons of histories, contemporaneous with and subsequent to the scenes of which I have written, wherein I have endeavored that candor should bar prejudice and *ex parte* statements give way to direct evidence.

It has been found that the proportion of unbiased testimony is small and of disinterested evidence still less as compared with the volume presented. This is, however, a natural sequence.

The Powers sought the overthrow of popular government, as a safeguard to monarchy. To them it appeared, at first, a matter of self-defense. They believed their own perpetuity menaced by the appearance of a Republic on the continent, and that danger was enhanced in proportion to the success of the French experiment.

Distrust led to estrangement, estrangement to deceit, deceit to intrigue and intrigue to hate. Their hatred was against popular government as a principle, then against France for espousing that principle, then against Napoleon as the representative and powerful head of the French nation, and, finally, after so many overwhelming defeats at his hand, their hate and fear culminated in a life and death struggle against Napoleon the man.

And when, at last, by a unanimity of voice unprecedented, the French people proclaimed Napoleon Emperor, so virulent had become their malignity that it became an absolute motive, and, instead of accepting the Empire as an olive branch, it was received as a new and greater offense by the Powers. In the words of Napoleon:

"Unmitigated hatred was their cause—
The force of arms alone could be their cure."

It is not strange, therefore, that the "historians" have tempered their words to the cause they represented; nor that the Bourbons should join in the general attack. To write the truth was to proclaim their own infamy.

The difficulties, however, in obtaining the facts of history under such circumstances are not insurmountable. In the cross-examination of witnesses the most carefully organized case is often thrown into confusion. Such a multitude of witnesses rarely agree. Disagreements lead to contradictions, and these to unguarded admissions, and these to forced concessions, and, when all of these are submitted to examination and comparison, under the white light of impartiality, the truths are revealed—the absolute facts stand in relief.

The theory that Napoleon was inspired by the idea that he was "The Child of Destiny" is scarcely sufficient, to my mind, to reconcile the strange events and seeming inconsistencies of his remarkable career. I have, therefore, assumed that he was possessed of no less hallucination than that his course was directed, or, rather, suggested by an actual presiding deity whom he personified as Fate. To her he conceived he bore a relation similar to that of Achilles to

Thetis, though recognizing in Fate one possessed of no less power than Jove himself.

I prefer the word *suggested*, as it is scarcely in keeping with the character of Napoleon that he would have submitted to more than this, even from the Immortals.

The affection of Napoleon for Josephine is beyond discussion. There is no recorded instance of a higher or tenderer, a madder love between husband and wife; and yet love, the strongest passion of humanity, was made to yield—an impossibility to Napoleon, had he not believed heaven and earth stood in waiting for his action.

To group the more important events in Napoleon's career, epitomising his life and elucidating his character, and to bring all within the compass of a play or an hour's reading, is the object of this production.

I have, it will be discovered, antedated and crowded events, and partially, or entirely, ignored many of the notable characters and remarkable achievements connected with Napoleon's history, since, with the stated object in view, this was demanded where matter so abounds.

Between Act IV and Act V, Napoleon achieved much of his unapproachable glory, and the period between the Coronation, Act V, Scene Second, and the Divorce, Act VI, Scene Fifth, was doubtless the most brilliant of his history ; but, for the purpose of condensation and of dramatic construction, the historical facts are omitted, to be alluded to later in the lines set down to the actors.

It will be observed that the play jumps from the Re-creation of the Army, after the disastrous Russian campaign, to St. Helena, and yet the intervening time was fraught with the most stirring scenes and important results of Napoleon's life. But what limits of a play were capable of the ovation received by Napoleon upon his return from Elba, or a portrayal of Waterloo ?

These and other obvious deviations from historical accuracy will not, it is trusted, diminish the pleasure the reader may find in these pages. In the main, they are true to history.

R. S. DEMENT,

Chicago, October, 1892.

PERSONS REPRESENTED.

NAPOLEON BONAPARTE, afterwards NAPOLEON I.
General of France, afterwards Emperor of France
CAULAINCOURT,   -   -   -   *Companion to Napoleon*
EUGENE DE BEAUHARNAIS, *Napoleon's adopted son, afterwards a Marshal of France*

NEY,
MURAT,
AUGEREAU,   }   -   -   -   -   *Marshals of France*
MASSENA,

MARSHAL BERTRAND,   } *Companions to Napoleon at St. Helena*
GENERAL MONTHOLON,

JOSEPH BONAPARTE,   }   -   -   *Brothers of Napoleon*
LUCIEN BONAPARTE,

CARNOT,   -   *Member of the Directory and friend of Napoleon*

BARRAS,
GOHIER,   }   -   *Members of the Directory and Conspirators*
MOULINS,

TALLEYRAND,
MOLÉ,
CAMBACERES,   }   -   -   -   -   *Ministers of France*
MONTALIVET,

METTERNICH,   -   -   -   -   -   *Minister of Austria*
VON COBLENTZ,   -   -   -   -   *Embassador of Austria*
MANFREDINI,   -   -   -   -   *Embassador of Tuscany*
ORIANI,   -   -   -   -   *An Astronomer*
SIR HUDSON LOWE,   -   -   -   *Governor of St. Helena*
MARCHAND,   -   -   -   *Napoleon's valet at St. Helena*
1ST AND 2D OFFICERS,   -   *Officers to Sir Hudson Lowe*
1ST, 2D AND 3D MEMBERS, *Of the Council of the Five Hundred*
1ST AND 2D CITIZENS.
1ST, 2D, 3D AND 4TH COURIERS.
JOSEPHINE,   *Wife of Napoleon, afterwards Empress of France*
THE PRINCESS AUGUSTA, *Affianced to Eugene, afterwards wife of Eugene*
MME. DE STAEL,   -   -   -   -   *Queen of the Salon*
1ST AND 2D MAIDS.

IN PANTOMIME.

PIUS VII., - - - - - - - *Pope of Rome*

DUROC, LEFEBVRE, SOULT,
DAVOUST, PONIATOWSKI,
MACDONALD, MORTIER,
DESAIX, KLEEBER, JUNOT, } - *Marshals and Generals of France*
LANNES, OUIDINOT,
BESSEIRES, JOUBERT,

GENERAL GOURGAND,
COUNT DE LAS CASAS,
DOCTOR O'MEARA, } - *Companions to Napoleon at St. Helena*
MME. LAS CASAS,
MME. BERTRAND,
MME. MONTHOLON,

REWBELL,
LETOURNEUR, } - *Members of the Directory*
LARAVEILLERE LEPEAUX,

1ST, 2D AND 3D SECRETARIES TO NAPOLEON.

FIVE CONSPIRATORS, PRELATES, A LITTLE GIRL, GENDARMES, SOLDIERS, CITIZENS.

NAPOLEON.

ACT I.—SCENE FIRST.

PARIS.

THE CONVENTION.

THE NIGHT OF THE TWELFTH VENDEMIAIRE.

Discovered—

Barras, Carnot, Gohier, Moulins, Joseph Bonaparte, Lepeaux, Letourneur, Rewell and other members.

(Barras Presiding.)

(Confusion.)

CARNOT.

IF that our edict seemed ill-timed,
   What boots it now, the Sections are in arms?

> *(Guns in distance.)*

Hark, to the booming of their cannonade!
Should not its thunder drown this senseless strife?

Continue we in this another day,
And that now muffled roar shall shake the dome.

MOULINS.

Let fall the dome! We ask but what is right,
And for that right will die if need be.

GOHIER.

There's worse than death—

JOSEPH BONAPARTE.

But, citizens—

GOHIER.

Shame !   Shame !
An' we are men, let us acquit us so !
An' we are dogs, who shall bewail our woe ?

JOSEPH BONAPARTE.

Even the instinct of the commonest cur
Would warn us of our danger now.

GOHIER.

Who will, then, let him tuck his tail and sneak
From the Convention.

CARNOT.

Are we but dogs, indeed,
That we should fall to whining at misfortune ?
Snap, snarl and catch each other at the throat
Until the Keeper of the Kennel comes
To lash us to our places ?

MOULINS.

Who is he
Whom you would style our Keeper ?

(*Enter 1st Courier.*)

BARRAS.

Now, here is one shall throw to you a bone.
Sirrah, Speak !

FIRST COURIER.

The Sections are victorious,
And everywhere do drive our soldiery.

(Exit Courier.)
(Confusion increases.)

LUCIEN BONAPARTE.

What, does our General sleep?   He has outlived
His usefulness.

GOHIER.

Now, is this brave, indeed,
To strike a Comrade in the back when most
He needs assistance?

LUCIEN BONAPARTE.

Nay, but to confront him—
Aye, strip him of command, ere he shall fall
And drag France down with him!

BARRAS.

Peace!   Peace!
(Enter Second Courier.)

Speak, Sirrah?

SECOND COURIER.

The Sections, like incarnate fiends,
Cut down our troops and sweep to victory!
Our soldiers are as chaff in a hurricane.

(Exit Courier.)
(Great confusion.)

BARRAS.

Such fury bodes not courage, but despair—
When once they're checked, they'll fly.

LUCIEN BONAPARTE.

"When once they're checked—"
But who is to check them? Not Menou.
                    (*Enter Third Courier.*)
Now shall we hear how they do "fly!"

BARRAS.
                    (*To Courier.*)
Speak, Sirrah, and catch breath after!

THIRD COURIER.

Our troops go over to the enemy
In whole battalions—those that remain
Are driven street by street!
                    (*Exit Courier.*)
        (*Confusion becomes indescribable.*)
            (*Enter Fourth Courier.*)

BARRAS.

Peace! Here is better news, I'll warrant you.

FOURTH COURIER.

Tidings from the General.
                (*Gives dispatch to Barras.*)

BARRAS.

            (*Tears open the dispatch and reads.*)

S' death! Damnable! Hell's furies seize him!
Menou grants an armistice.

                    (*Uproarious confusion.*)
            (*Enter Napoleon Bonaparte at-
            tended by three aids-de-camp.
            (*He advances to the President
            and seizes the dispatch.*)

BONAPARTE.

For France !
Lo ! I do rend this record of disgrace !
The sewers of Paris shall run red with blood
But that the White Waters of our France shall run
Unhindered to the Sea !—Give me command !

BARRAS.

Aye, be it so ! Let Bonaparte command !

ALL

Vive ! Vive le General ! Vive la Bonaparte !

BONAPARTE.

(*To First Aid-de-Camp.*)

Send Murat here !

(*Exit First Aid.*)

(*To Second Aid-de-Camp.*

Go you for Lannes !

(*Exit Second Aid.*)

(*To Third Aid-de-Camp.*)

You for Massena !

(*Exit Third Aid.*)

(*Enter Murat attended by First Aid.*)

(*To Murat.*)

Take your dragoons to Sablons and bring all
The artillery here ! I must have fifty guns,
And tumbrils, filled, to furnish them
With an hundred rounds of shell and ball !
These must be in place before the dawn !

(*Exit Murat.*)
(*Enter Lannes attended by Second Aid.*)

(To Lannes.)

Barricade the approaches and prepare
Your breastworks for our guns !

(Exit Lannes.)
(Enter Massena attended by Third Aid.)
(To Massena.)

Rally the troops
And form around the Tuileries !

(Exit Massena.)
(To the Convention.)

Now you may sleep,
And, with the morrow's breaking of the dawn,
When you again shall hear the cry, " To Arms ! "
" Down with the Convention ! " and " Destroy the Tyrants ! "
And hear the Sisters of the Guillotine
Shrieking for blood, be sure that blood shall come,
Attendant on the crash of grape and canister !
My guns will talk for France and there shall be
No answer to their voice except the dying wails
Of crushed conspirators !

ALL.

Vive ! Vive le General ! Vive la Bonaparte !

ACT I.—Scene Second.

Headquarters of General Bonaparte.

Discovered—

Barras, Gohier and Moulins.

Moulins.

OUR Bonaparte did make swift work of it.

Barras.

It was a bloody, bloody victory—
And horrible!

Gohier.

The Thirteenth Vendemiaire
Will not be soon forgot.

Moulins.

I am heart-sick
To think of it.

Gohier.

The people fell
Before the murderous artillery
Like blades o' grass to the mower.

MOULINS.

And now all France would worship the destroyer.

GOHIER.

Yes, we are naught beside him with the people.

(The Princess Augusta is discovered.)

BARRAS.

We ? Aye, and every one, it would appear.
In France there's but one man.

MOULINS.

And he a Corsican !

GOHIER.

That yesterday
Was but a corporal.   Our generals
Are quite forgot in presence of this stripling.

MOULINS.

But, gentlemen, we may not quite despise him.

BARRAS.

He grows too fast—we'll nip him in good time,
Ere this green fruitage of his glory
Shall ripen into power.

GOHIER.

But how ?
The task will scarcely prove an easy one.

BARRAS.

Now shall we post him off to Italy—
Once there we'll hold him to our purposes.

MOULINS.

But if he should o'erwhelm the allied arms?

BARRAS.

Impossible!

MOULINS.

I'm not so sure of it.

BARRAS.

Well, then, 'twere easy to dispatch him.
What, are you grave?   We'll trip this Corporal General,
Never fear, or make him one of us.

(*Exeunt.*)

(*Enter Napoleon Bonaparte.*)

BONAPARTE.

'Tis said that when these eyes first saw the light,
They gazed upon a piece of tapestry,
Whereon were painted Ilium's tragic scenes ;
And that my father, on the bed of death,
In words prophetic cried :
"Napoleon—the glory of a greater France !"
   Ah, Fame, thou Ignis-Fatuus of Pride,
Thou canst not tempt me from that nobler destiny !
Fate hath decreed the glory of Her son.
   Between Her visits on my natal hour
The Mystic Numbers alternate—
   The clustering years, in coronals of stars,
Flame in the crown She holds above my head.
   Seven and three and five and seven and three—
The divination of the Unity !
I'll doubt no more !   *Jacta est alea !*

Fate, Supreme Goddess, hail !
Lo, let the firm alliance now be sealed !
Lead on ! Lead on !
              About it now, good brain,
Thou never-resting, we are dauntless now !
Conceive and She shall execute
The Indomitable Will !
                      (Enter Augusta.)
Princess !

AUGUSTA.

Art quite alone ?

BONAPARTE.

Why, yes, my pretty one.

AUGUSTA.

Go not to Italy !

BONAPARTE.

Ah, my fond bride
Hath sent thee ?

AUGUSTA.

No, no ! General, go not !
Here at thy feet, I pray that thou go not !

BONAPARTE.

What ! Has Barras again affronted thee ?

AUGUSTA.

Not mine ! Not mine ! But thine the danger now.

BONAPARTE.

From Barras ? I, in danger ? Oh, no, no !
Barras harms but the weak and powerless.

He'd dare not even meet thy courage, child.
But, tell me, has he importuned thee ?

AUGUSTA.

He has twice approached me since I saw thee last,
To prate me of his suit and yet this hour,
Within this very room, I overheard
The soulless wretch, with Moulins and Gohier,
Plotting thy overthrow.

BONAPARTE.

Thou heardst them, here ?

AUGUSTA.

I came to bear thy sweet wife's compliments
Touching the matter which this note imparts,

(Gives letter.)

And played the eavesdropper.

BONAPARTE.

Rather, the friend.

AUGUSTA.

Heard I but the conclusion of their council.
They spake of the Thirteenth Vendemiaire,
And called thee butcher, monster and the like ;
Prated of their own qualities, the while,
And darkly hinted of a villainous plot
For thy swift overthrow ; failing in which,
Thy no less swift dispatch.

BONAPARTE.

Heardst thou the plot?

AUGUSTA.

They, seemingly, had been discussing that
Before I came—I got no clue to it.

BONAPARTE.

So—So—'Think'st thou couldst play a part for me?

AUGUSTA.

Prove me! Oh, wouldst thou prove me!

BONAPARTE.

I will!
Thou'dst be a soldier's bride—I'll prove thee,
I'll set thee on to unravel this Barras
And knit him up again into a glove
That we shall wear to our own purposes.

AUGUSTA.

Barras!

BONAPARTE.

Ah, fear him not! I'll counsel thee.
'Tis well that he has marked thee for his prey—
We'll lead him to the precipice—And yet—

AUGUSTA.

And yet—

BONAPARTE.

I do regret in this to employ thee—
Thou'rt young to learn dissimulation.

AUGUSTA.

I should be young, indeed, if still untaught
In such diplomacy. In other lands

'Tis, doubtless, otherwise ; but here, in France,
We are nothing not *en masque.*
I pray thee give me leave to prove myself
A worthy damoiselle of La Belle France.

BONAPARTE.

I'd show thee worthy in a worthier cause,
But that I know thou needest not the showing.
Ah, this will try thy strength !

AUGUSTA.

Try me ?

BONAPARTE.

Thou'lt find more thorns than roses in thy path.

AUGUSTA.

In such a cause, send me through thorns alone.

BONAPARTE.

I will, since it must be so, and at once.
Know, then, the first step to our purposes
Must lie in the offense of thy heart's love.
Barras 's no fool although he is a villain ;
He knows thy choice of Eugene—knows that thou
Art pure and good ; too noble in thy nature
To stoop to wrong.   Now he must see thee break
Thy bond with Eugene.   He'd not believe
Less than his eyes in such a happening.

AUGUSTA.

But Eugene must know all—

BONAPARTE.

'   That were defeat.
Eugene could play no part less than his own—
I will tell him all in Italy.

AUGUSTA.

But if he dare some rash extremity?

BONAPARTE.

Then shall we in extremities o'er match him.
We'll place him under friendly surveillance.

AUGUSTA.

But to himself—

BONAPARTE.

He is too noble to destroy himself.

AUGUSTA.

I will do it—

BONAPARTE.

Eugene will dearer prize thee when he knows.
Now to our plans! When Barras sees thee break
With Eugene, for his own fair prospering suit
He'll hold thee kindred to his confidence.
Be not in haste—he'll come to thee anon
And, in good time, for all our purposes.
Then shalt thou play him plot with counterplot.

AUGUSTA.

Command me!

BONAPARTE.

Win Barras speedily—

(She offers to go.)

Stay!   In thy coiffure wear this ornament.

(Places stiletto in her hair.)

If he prove gallant, treat him gallantly.

AUGUSTA.

Life is a precious thing—

BONAPARTE.

Thine honor, child,
Is worth whole hecatombs of lives.

ACT I.—SCENE THIRD.

PARIS.

SALON OF MME. DE STAEL.

Discovered—

> Barras, Gohier, Moulins and Generals.
> Ladies and Gentlemen.
> Mme. De Stael.

>   (*Enter Eugene and Augusta.*)

DE STAEL.

G ENERAL—Princess—you are right welcome !

EUGENE.

Madame, yours is a royal greeting.

DE STAEL.

My guests are royal—the best blood of France.

EUGENE.

You honor us.

DE STAEL.

That were impossible.

EUGENE.

But we have not all proved our quality—
In blood, alone, honors sit idly by.

De Stael.

Brave youth and glorious maidenhood
Precede great deeds.

Barras.

(Who has approached Augusta.)

Fair Princess, thou wast ne'er so wondrous fair,
Yet ever wast thou quite beyond compare!

Augusta.

Now thou wouldst prove the flatterer, I think.

Barras.

Believe me and spurn not my heart's devotion!
I'd give my life to prove it true to thee.
Count me among thy slaves and I shall be
The happiest of men.

Augusta.

My slaves?   My slaves!
(Laughing.)

Barras.

Then name me with thy worshipers.

Augusta.

I have but one.

Barras.

And he?

Augusta.

Not he, but she—my grandmother.

BARRAS.

Would that same grand-dam were an armored knight.
I'd try conclusions with him, though he were
A Cœur de Leon!   And dost thou, then, love?

AUGUSTA.

I love the Corsican—

BARRAS.

As all do who love France.
But, tell me, now, hast thou but jests for me?
(Augusta shows confusion.)
Thou bidst me hope!   I live in ecstacy!
Wear this for me.

*(He takes a rose from his coat and
gives it to her.   She hesitates, then
takes it and fastens it on her
breast.   Eugene, who has seen
all, shows anger.)*
(Enter Bonaparte and Josephine.)

DE STAEL.

General, Madame, you ennoble us!

(Bonaparte goes to Eugene.)

JOSEPHINE.

How beautiful it is!

(Regarding the Salon.)

DE STAEL.

Yours will be magnificent!

JOSEPHINE.

Mine?

DE STAEL.

The Tuileries.

JOSEPHINE.

Pardon me!

DE STAEL.

I speak most earnestly.
The General will bring all to your feet.

JOSEPHINE.

Your fair opinion honors him, madame.

DE STAEL.

Ah, you should be the happiest of women!
Such opportunities, such power yours,
To mold great destinies!

JOSEPHINE

And I am happy
When in my happiness I can lend happiness
To others.

DE STAEL.

Ah, in this, all France indebted
Stands to you, madame—

JOSEPHINE.

No, not "indebted"—there can be no debt—
Love only proves itself when it has reached
The last extremity for whom it loves.

DE STAEL.

A lofty sentiment!—You go to Italy?

JOSEPHINE.

The General fears so much fatigue for me.

DE STAEL.

So great and yet so ardent in his love !

(*Laughing.*

Your Salon, then, shall cheat his absence
And be gayest in all Paris.

JOSEPHINE.

I court repose.

DE STAEL.

Ambition's consort
May not know repose. The highest talents, art,
In statecraft, here find possibilities—
The Salon is greater than the Council.
Here one may make and unmake kings
At will, build thrones or banish dynasties.
Here woman may attain her ends.

JOSEPHINE.

Happy attainment rarely comes to us
When selfishness suggests the motive.

DE STAEL.

There is no action with self motive gone.
Let us rail not against our being's law,
Or chaos comes again. What say the saints?
That we are made, in that the Maker
Should be glorified.

JOSEPHINE.

The Creator's glory
Lies in the possibilities that wait
Upon created ones.

(*Bonaparte approaches.*)

DE STAEL.

Ah! General,
You join us?

(Shows confusion.)

JOSEPHINE.

We were discussing the Salon.

BONAPARTE.

The Salon is a menace, constantly,
To the stability of government.

DE STAEL.

Is it, then, true you are not fond of ladies,
General?

BONAPARTE.

I am very fond of my wife.

*(They are approached by Barras
and Augusta. Bonaparte and
Josephine go up stage to meet
them.)*

DE STAEL.

(Aside.)

How is it that I tremble in his presence?
Scarce speak—Scarce breathe—Is he a demigod?
And I am she who rules the half of France!
Rules by her will—Her power over men!
And this man, this, inspires me with awe—
Affrights me!
Sees he into my soul? An' if he should,
There is no murder there! Why, this is weakness—
I'll master me or pluck out both mine eyes!
But what though I were sightless? I should feel
His presence! Ah!—I will tear out my heart
Or conquer me!

EUGENE.

(*To Augusta.*)

Monsieur Barras is entertaining, quite.

AUGUSTA.

(*To Eugene.*)

Oh, we have planned great politics and statecraft!

(*Laughing.*)

EUGENE.

It would appear so.

AUGUSTA.

Forgive me! Eugene—
Monsieur Barras awaits.

EUGENE.

(*Aside.*)

Death !—
A brilliant life will, haply, shorter be,
Even as a falling star whose life goes out
When its effulgence most attracts our view ;
So shall my glory through this little world
Blaze like a meteor in the firmament
And then go out forever. Oh, farewell,
Farewell, Augusta ! Now am I resolved.

DE STAEL.

(*Approaching Bonaparte.*)

General, I trust our ladies' presence
Shall rest you from the burdens of the Camp.

BONAPARTE.

Our wits are often put to greater straits
In the Salon than on the battle field.

DE STAEL.

But here, at least, are conquests bloodless.

BONAPARTE.

And heartless !

DE STAEL.

You have tripped my words—I was not clever—
But tell me, now, do you ne'er have remorse
For the Thirteenth Vendemiaire?

BONAPARTE.

Madame,
That was my seal—the seal Fate stamped on France.
Europe shall yet attest it.

DE STAEL.

Our women souls
May only know the right, and cannot rise
To the Olympian philosophy.
The dead are dead to us, and all the gods
Cannot return them to our love and homes.

BONAPARTE.

What, then, is death?   Gateway for noble souls
To higher possibilities.   Others reck not
Save as among the wastes o' the universe.
Fate wills that some of us remain awhile
To do her bidding.   Madame, what is your task ?

DE STAEL.

I trust 'tis not to kill.

BONAPARTE.

Amen !

JOSEPHINE.

(*Approaching.*)

My love!

BONAPARTE.

I attend you.

DE STAEL.

Will you not dance?

JOSEPHINE.

The General must rest.

(*Exeunt Bonaparte and Josephine.*)

TABLEAU.

THE DANCE.

EUGENE REGARDING BARRAS AND AUGUSTA.

NAPOLEON.

ACT II.—SCENE FIRST.

PARIS.

DRAWING ROOM OF HOTEL ELBOEF.

Barras Discovered.

> (*Enter the Princess Augusta,
> disguised as a page. With
> four other pages.*)

BARRAS.

PERDITION snatch me quick, but ye are choice.
And yet have I no time for ye to-day.

> (*Exit pages.*)

Stay ! Stay ! Marie, I had forgot myself.
What's that I'd taste next to thy pretty lips ?
Go fetch it, straight, my love.

> (*Exit Marie.*)

The Corsican
Is yet far in advance in spite of me.
He strides the earth a very demigod.

> (*Re-enter Marie with wine.*)

> (*To Marie.*)

I'll see thee presently.   (*Exit Marie.*)
With cunning spies, lodged i' the midst o' the camp,
Have I beset him, and still no clue
With which to humble him, scarcely annoy.

> (*Drinks.*)

I strike him through the journals
And, as his victories come heralded,

I intercept reports to temper them,
And, yet, by some means, truth will leak,
And through the streets no other sound is heard
But that same damned, inexorable yell :
"Vive le Bonaparte !"

(Enter Gohier and Moulins.)
(Cries without,
"Vive le Bonaparte.")

What means this, Gohier ?   Are the people mad ?

Gohier.

The streets are thronging with the multitude,
Splitting their throats with "Vive le Bonaparte,"
And yet 'tis scarce an hour they've had the news.

Barras.

You mean from Generals Junot and Eugene?
Prate they to the populace ere we
Receive them in the Directory?

Gohier.

The standards and rich trophies they have brought
Attract attention.   The people guess the rest.

Barras.

We'll set them guessing presently.

Gohier.

Nor can we long delay.   This blazing brand
Of glory he has snatched, fires all hearts
And will illume the world unless put out.

Barras.

Now he'll to Paris,
Borne as world's conqueror amidst a sea

Of crazy-witted fools whose rotten breaths
In loud acclaim shall roll in mighty waves
Before him.

GOHIER.

An' we permit it, yes.

BARRAS.

Permit!
"Permit" is good.

(Rings.   Re-enter Augusta
disguised as a page bearing
wine. Exit—stops and over-
hears what follows.)

"Permit" is very good,
Upon my faith—it smacks of enterprise.   *(They drink.)*
An' you have mettle, gentlemen, we'll try
Conclusions with this young "Achilles," soon.

BARRAS AND MOULINS.

(Touching glasses.)

Here's to our mettle!

GOHIER.

Two hundred thousand pounds
In yellow gold await emergencies.

(Sensation.)

BARRAS.

From whence?

GOHIER.

Why not across the channel?

BARRAS.

Methods legitimate have sadly failed.

MOULINS.

And ever will fail 'gainst this Corsican.

BARRAS.

Is't tangible, this sum?   Does't wait us?   Where?

GOHIER.

In the Bank of England.

BARRAS.

To whose order?
Or in whose name stands it accredited?

GOHIER.

Mine.

BARRAS.

The conditions?

GOHIER.

As we shall choose to make them.
The gold awaits us, that I warrant you.

BARRAS.

Well, you would prove us—

GOHIER.

Good!   And so will I.
This sum magnificent insures success
An' we set to it—that you'll not dispute.
'Tis but a question, then, of action, means,
Scruples, et cætera.

BARRAS.

Pray you, go on !
We are committed touching the Legitimate.

GOHIER.

What shall "Legitimate" infer?

BARRAS.

Bribes, lies and so forth.   Mark you, twixt right and wrong
In war, the line's a faint one, and we draw it
Fainter and fainter in extremities.
We are not wit-strangers—pray you, go on !

GOHIER.

Well, then, have at you, gentlemen !   Attend.
The Corsican is wanted by our cousins,
Albeit they care not for his trunk and legs.

BARRAS.

Well, well, go on!

GOHIER.

I've ta'en some action,
Feeling assured of your good offices,
To this extent, Monsieur Botot awaits us.

BARRAS.

Well, well?

GOHIER.

Arrest " Achilles" and confine him close,
Then hold him to our secret order.

BARRAS.

But how, and when?   You speak in parables.

GOHIER.

Occasions will prove ample.   When he comes,
Borne as a conqueror, he'll fear no danger.
Come! Botot awaits.

(Exeunt.)

ACT II.—SCENE SECOND.

DRAWING ROOM OF MME. BONAPARTE.

————

(*Enter Barras.*)

BARRAS.

BY Juno, now this Bonaparte
    Has left rich pasturage for some man's colt!
    I'll look to it.   Who has a better right?
I helped him to his greatness, 'tis but just
He should repay me.   And I'll prescribe the terms;
My choice of coin.   I'll not take the Republic's
But that of Royalty less circulate—
Recently new stamped but not impaired.
Oh, good Botot, Petit Achilles trip
And leave to me his fair Briseis!

(*Enter the Princess Augusta.*)

AUGUSTA.

You've been kept waiting—I regret it, sir.

BARRAS.

An untimely call—the affairs of state
In these most busy and eventful times
Demand us unawares.

AUGUSTA.

Have you advice from Italy?

BARRAS.

And it shall please you, yes.
This letter. 'Tis for Madame Bonaparte,
And from the General. I came at once
Upon receiving it, to her, and beg
If any further service I can lend—

(Gives letter.)

AUGUSTA.

She will be pleased the happiness to grant
Of such employment. I shall in my best words
Report you, monsieur. But tell me, now,
Came you upon this business solely?

BARRAS.

You know it was my Princess I would meet.

AUGUSTA.

The fair Briseis?

BARRAS.

Ha! Have you played a jealous listener?

AUGUSTA.

I heard you speak the word as I did enter.
Is it for this that you have made me false
To my great benefactor and my lover?
It serves me well!

BARRAS.

My Princess, do you weigh me
'Gainst a word, not knowing what 'twas coupled with?
By all the Immortals now, 'tis I am wronged.

AUGUSTA.

Oh, I have been fond of thee, alas !

(*Feigns to weep.*)

BARRAS.

Now, by white faith, I have made tardy footing—
Two years' devotion yields to one weak word.

AUGUSTA.

What was't thou said'st then ?   Tell me, tell me, love !

BARRAS.

What could I say, sweet love, but in sweet love ?
I was but making merry with the times—
Comparing thee, so far beyond compare,
With this half-widowed fair Briseis here—
Thou heard'st me laugh at the comparison ?

AUGUSTA.

(*Faintly.*)

And was that all ?

BARRAS.

She's coming—I must go—
I could not bear to look upon her now
Since she has been the subject of thy grief.
Farewell.

(*He kisses her hand and exits.
She smiles upon him as he goes
off, rubs vigorously the hand
he has kissed with her handker-
chief, which she then tosses into
the fire.*)

AUGUSTA.

Pah !

(*Enter Josephine.*)

JOSEPHINE.

He is gone ?

AUGUSTA.

I loathe him !

JOSEPHINE.

But he must not suspect it.

AUGUSTA.

Oh, no— He brings letters to you.
(*Gives letter and exits.*)

JOSEPHINE.   (*Reading.*)

"Junot takes to Paris twenty-two standards. You will
come back with him, will you not? Misery without reme-
dy, sorrow without comfort, unmitigated anguish, will be
my portion if it is my misfortune to see him come back
alone, my own adored wife ! He will breathe at your
shrine and perhaps you will even grant him the unsurpassed
privilege of kissing your cheek. And I will be far, far
away !

You will come, here at my side, to my heart, in my arms !
Take wings, come ! Come ! Yet journey slowly—the
road is long, bad, fatiguing. If some calamity should hap-
pen—if the exertion—

Set out at once, my beloved one, but travel slowly.

NAPOLEON."

Will I come to thee? Ask thou the flower
If it will turn its fond face to the Sun !
Even as the soul would swiftly take its flight
Unto the source of its supremest ecstacy,
I come, my love, I come !
(*Enter Eugene, in uniform.*)
Eugene !
(*They embrace.*)

How long since you left Italy ?

EUGENE.

I came with Joseph Bonaparte, Junot,
And the escort that our fair trophies brought.
Your letter, too.

JOSEPHINE.

How fares the General?

EUGENE.

Did he not, then, inform you?

JOSEPHINE.

Oh, yes : but, tell me.
Is he indeed well, quite well, dear Eugene?

EUGENE.

He was in perfect health on my departure.

JOSEPHINE.

And do you keep a close watch over him?

EUGENE.

There's not a soldier would not die for him.
But you are worn and weary, mother dear—
What, are you ill?

JOSEPHINE.

Oh, no, not ill, not ill—
Nor weary in the cause I am intrusted—
But 'tis a time we may not hope for rest.
I may be summoned any moment hence—
Conspiracy is newly footed.

EUGENE.

Ah,

We shall baffle them !

JOSEPHINE.

If we are quick enough.
Oh, Eugene, it is well you are with us—

EUGENE.

How, now ?

(*Enter a page.*)

PAGE.

Madame Therese de Talien.

(*Exit page.*)

JOSEPHINE.

'Tis urgent—wait my return!—

(*Exit Josephine.*)

EUGENE.

France, thou art safe while thou canst boast such women.

(*Re-enter Augusta.*)

AUGUSTA.

My love !

EUGENE.

My darling.

(*They embrace.*)

AUGUSTA.

You do forgive me?

EUGENE.

Forgive ! Forgive you ? Oh, 'twas sweet revenge
To make Barras your plaything and our servant.
I have paid dearly for your cleverness—

AUGUSTA.

Pray you no more!—
How slowly have the hours dragged, Eugene!
Yet am I paid for all a thousand times
In this fair moment on your loving breast.

EUGENE.

How at your feet I used to sit, the while
I told, in fondest words I knew, my love,
And held up fairest pictures of the life
In store for us!
What happy visions rose before us!
But none to equal this reality.
There was one look you gave to me at times—
A look you could not give unto another—
There! There! Again does it enrapture me!
Oh, my darling!
How that one look has nestled in my heart
Through all the weary hours of absence!
How has it cheered me when all else was vain!
How like a light from heaven illumed my path
And as a beacon brought me back to you!

AUGUSTA.

Speak on, that I may hear the music sweet
Of your dear voice! It has been long, so long,
Since I have listened to it, love! Speak on!

EUGENE.

Your beauty robs me of my words—
What eloquence could rise to such a theme!
On yester-night, dear love, I dreamed a dream,—
A lovely dream, but not so fair as this.

AUGUSTA.

Pray, tell it me!

EUGENE.

A sunlit vale
Where perfumed grasses were all interspersed
With flowers rare and rich.   Sweet mignonette
And heliotrope, innumerable roses
And nameless flowers as redolent.
And there were little bowers of jessamine
Whose balmy breath is but less sweet, dear love,
Than that wherein your kisses nestle.
All these did freight
Soft zephyrs that floated through the glen
And circled round my head in eddying swirl.
There seemed a melody of song to rise
From grass and flower and the birds caught this
And carried it into the higher measures
Of their dulcet strains.   Then it did echo
Through the glen, till, following adown
The fringes of the gentle winding stream,
That ran just through the center of the vale,
It lost itself upon the boundless sea.

AUGUSTA.

How beautiful!

EUGENE.

Here and there were quiet little nooks
And fair retreats, 'neath denser foliage
In every hue and matchless tint of green.
And some old trees, staid warders of the vale,
Were rich with clambering roses,
Clematis sweet, that graced their massive trunks,
Or other vines luxuriant,

That sought the very topmost bending boughs
To peep out first in lovelier blossom
And catch the morning glory of the sun.

AUGUSTA.

Dear, dear Eugene.

EUGENE.

Fair clouds
Were ever blushing in divinest tints,
Casting their mellow shadows on the vale,
And but one charm was wanting.

AUGUSTA.

And that?

EUGENE.

Your presence, darling, then't had nothing lacked
Of heaven for Eugene.

(Re-enter Josephine.)

JOSEPHINE.

Oh, England ! England !

EUGENE.

How, now?

JOSEPHINE.

Even now as ever since this base King George
Has been the tool of baser counsellors.

EUGENE.

Impart !

JOSEPHINE.

Led by the crafty Barras and Gohier
The plot awaits swift consummation.

AUGUSTA.

Has Barras, then, been cleverer than we ?

EUGENE.

What plot is this?

JOSEPHINE.

Has not Augusta told you?

AUGUSTA.

Not yet—I—I—we had not time for it yet—

EUGENE.

Nay, dear, the fault was mine—pray you, delay
No longer!

AUGUSTA.

Know, then, 'tis planned to bribe the General's guard
And basely thus make him a prisoner.
Two hundred thousand pounds is pledged
To the enterprise.

JOSEPHINE.

And M. Botot
Is sent a secret messenger this day
To dispatch it.

AUGUSTA.

Today? Then does Barras
Suspect, and plays a part with me! So—So—
'Tis part for part! Mme. de Talien,
Where is she?

JOSEPHINE.

Ere this, at home, I warrant—
She'll have another meeting with Botot.

EUGENE.

We must move swiftly in this matter now—
To what extent can she command this fellow?

JOSEPHINE.

To absolute control.   For, know, he is
At once a pliable and simple fool
In presence of a pretty woman.

EUGENE.

Who, then, is implicated?

JOSEPHINE.

           We shall acquaint
You presently.

EUGENE.

I'll hasten our report of victories,
And then, my mother, we must both set out
For Italy.   We shall be with the General
Ere Botot has made half the journey.
But you, Augusta, will remain in Paris
To keep us well informed.   A weighty trust
We dare not risk to another.

                         (*Exeunt.*)

ACT II.—SCENE THIRD.

PALACE OF THE LUXEMBOURG.

THE DIRECTORY.

Discovered—

Carnot, Barras, Lepeaux, Rewbell, Letourneur,
Secretaries and Gendarmes, &c.

Carnot Presiding.

CARNOT.

(Continuing his speech.)

LET us, then, not forget
 That these successes, from the first so great,
 They have astounded Christendom,
Reflect the genius solely of our General.
He found an army miserably clad,
Relaxed in discipline, ambitionless,
Cursing their country and no less themselves
For its neglect, their own torpidity ;
Five and thirty thousand of such soldiery
Was all he had with which to meet the foe.
And such a foe! Shall I recall its strength?
England, Austria, Bavaria, Piedmont,
Naples and some minor states of Germany,
And Italy—all joined to Austria's league.
Its armies, skilled in every art of war,
Well fed, well clothed, well paid, brave in success,
And ably generaled.

What glory sits upon our Eagles now !
Our armies newly armed, fed, clothed and paid
From spoils of the enemy, challenge
The admiration of the enlightened world !
While those proud thrones that banded their great strength
To crush the young Republic, now, amazed,
Stand trembling for their own security !

(Enter page.)

PAGE.

Generals Joseph Bonaparte, Junot and Beauharnais.

CARNOT.

Immediately admit them.   *(Exit page.)*
*(Enter Joseph Bonaparte, Junot
and Eugene, attended by Gendarmes bearing standards.)*

Citizen-Generals :
In the name of France and the People
The Directory welcomes you.

EUGENE.

Citizen-President and Directors :
The General of France sends, greeting you,
Trophies of victory from Italy,
And here would lay them at your feet
As at the shrine of France.

CARNOT.

We attend most eagerly.

EUGENE.

*(Taking the flag upon which
was inscribed the bulletin.)*

He has indeed great victories to report
And on our flag inscribes this bulletin.

(Reads from one side of flag.)

"To the Army of Italy, the grateful country."

(Reads from other side of flag.)

"115000 prisoners, 170 standards, 550 pieces of battering cannon, 600 pieces of field artillery, 5 bridge equipages, 9 sixty-four gun ships, 12 thirty-two gun frigates, 12 corvettes, 18 galleys.

"Armistice with the King of Sardinia, Convention with Genoa, Armistice with the Duke of Parma, Armistice with the King of Naples, Armistice with the Pope. Preliminaries of Leoben, Convention of Montebello with the Republic of Genoa. Treaty of peace with the Emperor at Campo Formio, Liberty given to the people of Bologna, Ferrara, Modena, Massa-Carara, La Romagna, Lombardy, Bressera, Bormio, the Vallentina, the Genoese, the Imperial Fiefs, the people of the departments of Coreigra, of the Ægean Sea and of Ithaca. Sent to Paris master-pieces of Michael Angelo, of Genercino, of Titian, of Paul Veronese, of Correggio, of Albano, of Corracei, of Raphael and of Leonardo da Vinci."

(During the reading of the report Carnot is greatly excited. As it progresses all rise to their feet. Carnot comes down from his chair. Tearing his cloak open at the conclusion of the report, he displays a miniature of Napoleon, which he has worn concealed there, and holds it up as he addresses Joseph Bonaparte.)

CARNOT.

Tell your brother
That I do wear him next unto my heart!

(Turns to Directors.)

Go fire your guns! Ring wildly every bell!

Scream with the fife! Let the shrill bugle tell,
With clang of steel and the unmuffled drum
And loud huzzas, that victory has come!
Fire, fire your guns! Let deep-toned thunder roll
Throughout great France, filling each patriot soul
With Victory's shouts, uprising from the heart,
Vive la Republic! Vive le Bonaparte!

ALL.

Vive la Republic!   Vive le Bonaparte!

———————

SHOUTING, CANNON, BELLS AND DRUMS WITHOUT.

SCENE CHANGES

TO

PARIS ILLUMINATED.

JOSEPHINE.

ACT III.—SCENE FIRST.

MILAN.

DRAWING ROOM OF THE PALACE SERBELLONI.

Bonaparte and Caulaincourt.
Discovered reading.

BONAPARTE.

CONTEMPTIBLE!
That this should be permitted is most strange ;
For we are France.

CAULAINCOURT.

Their silence proves
The sympathy of the Directory.

BONAPARTE.

Are they so blinded to the interests
Of France, nay, even their own interests
Most selfish, as to let their jealousy
Creep in and so despoil them, utterly,
Of all the vantage they might borrow
From the lustre of my star ?   They cannot think
That I will patiently endure this ?
Do they not realize that I have power
To crush them ?
(Crushes paper and takes another.)
Here's language bears the imprint of Barras—

His very words! Can it be possible
He should be such a peevish bungler
As to permit his very tricks of speech
To thus betray him? So—So—

CAULAINCOURT.

I now recall what you once said of him.

BONAPARTE.

Well—

CAULAINCOURT.

These were your words:
That man, whose keenest satisfaction
Lies in the persecution of his foe,
Can have no friend he would not sacrifice.
Though he your shoe may buckle day by day,
'Tis only that you wear it out for him.
Such friendship rests upon subserviency.

BONAPARTE.

I could not trust him.

CAULAINCOURT.

I have found rare pastime
In despising him.

BONAPARTE.

That is unworthy of you,
Caulaincourt: great souls stoop not to rancor.
Nor this, nor envy, dwells within the hearts
Of the truly great. In youth 'tis pardoned,
But to be outgrown. These wasps may sting us
And the sting may burn—there's poison in it—
So, it may fret the skin, but that is all.

(Reads.)

" He keeps the plunder." To whom do they allude?
" He does affect a heartless despotism,
Overrides all law! " Rare rhetoricians !
To "affect !" To "affect despotism !"
What masterly envenomed slander that !
I like the knaves and will requite them.
 I am humiliated when I feel
They have the power to annoy me.
Ah ! It is the little things that fret
And so disturb us, more than all else,
In the vicissitudes of life.
Let us look above, beyond them.
Who lives the butt and sport of daily circumstance
Is no more than a moth, in sunbeam basking,
To idly drift, before a vagrant zephyr,
On to the little death that waits him.
Philosophy is the one source of strength ;
For he who can despise or grief or joy,
With will indomitable, pressing on,
Unto the goal of his ambition, wins.
Were't not that he must eat and sleep, I'd say
A man might come to be great.

(Enter Josephine and Eugene in wraps.)

Josephine !

JOSEPHINE.

(Falls in his arms.)

My love !

BONAPARTE.

Why, she has fainted !
Eugene cannot speak ! What can this mean ?

EUGENE.

That we have saved you.

BONAPARTE.

Saved us? From whom? What?

EUGENE.

The blackest of conspiracies.

BONAPARTE.

Well—Well—

EUGENE.

A princely sum is set to bribe your guard
And make you an unlawful prisoner.

BONAPARTE.

To bribe my guard? Golconda could not do it!
And is that all?

EUGENE.

No—No—I'll tell you all.
Meantime, be sure of those about you.
Look to my mother!

BONAPARTE.

(Regarding Josephine.)

Now, if I live, the knaves shall answer this!

ACT III.—SCENE SECOND.

MILAN.

PALACE OF SERBELLONI.

A Large Salon, Divided into Three Rooms by Marble Columns.

Discovered—

In room farthest back :
Military Officers and group of Ladies and Gentlemen.
In middle room :
Josephine and Ladies of rank, Marshals and Generals,
Murat, Massena, Duroc, Ney, Lannes, Besseires, Desaix, Kleeber,
Augereau and Eugene.

———

*(Enter in front room Bona-
parte and Caulaincourt.)*
*(Caulaincourt passes into second
room. Josephine comes down
centre and joins Bonaparte in
front room.)*

JOSEPHINE.

MY love !

BONAPARTE.

(Regarding her.)

Now had Apollo patterned from thy mold,
His daughters had been lovelier !
Nay, could I pick from out the universe,

Other than thee, though dowered with a world,
Witness, sweet heaven, I would not change my choice !

> (*He presses her hand to his lips;
> then leads her up stage and is
> met by Eugene, Caulaincourt,
> Ney, Augereau, Murat, Mas-
> sena, Lannes and Desaix, who
> come into front room.*)

AUGEREAU.

Have you made answer to the Duke of Parma?

BONAPARTE.

The Duke of Parma is unfortunate ;
But, left where he is now, will do no harm,
And, doubtless, will serve well our purposes.

AUGEREAU.

But he is a Bourbon, General.

BONAPARTE.

Well, then, he is a Bourbon !
Has nature, therefore, gifted him the less?
Is't so despicable a family ?

> (*Sensation.*)

Because three Bourbons have been killed in France,
Follows it we must hunt the others down ?
Can'st punish France for the crimes of the Sans Culottes?
Proscriptions falling thus upon a name,
A family, a class, I shall not approve.

AUGEREAU.

The Bourbons plot continually against you.

BONAPARTE.

And, if they do? May they, then, not be won?
They are Frenchmen.

MASSENA.

To be a Frenchman—

NEY.

Is glorious! And stranger to defeat.

MURAT.

War is the grandest of professions!

BONAPARTE.

War is horrible! You can bear witness
I ever courted peace, save in dishonor.
My tastes were for the arts and sciences;
My joy, the full prosperity of France.
War is the resort of Barbarism!

MURAT.

Are we, then, barbarians?

BONAPARTE.

Not so.
We have but fought in righteous self-defense.
The allied powers of despotism sought
To crush the Republic. We have vanquished them,
And are invaders, through necessity.
You all know I have oft implored for peace,
Aye, even on the battle-field, when victory
Perched with our eagles. Their answer
Has been insult and new coalitions

Of the Powers.　In less than one year's time,
Have they not sent five powerful armies
To o'erwhelm us?
Each several army we have quite destroyed
And then have honorably plead for peace.
Still, 'tis denied us, and we can but fight.

(*Enter Oriani attended.*)

(*To Oriani.*)

Monseigneur, you are welcome!

ORIANI.

Ah! General, this magnificence
With which you are surrounded dazes me!

BONAPARTE.

Can it be such miserable splendors blind
A man who every night does contemplate
The far more lofty and impressive glories
Of the skies?

(*Enter Manfredini attended.*)

(*To Manfredini.*)

And can we serve your Grand Duke?

MANFREDINI.

Before the conqueror of Italy,
The General most excellent of France,
Most humbly does our Grand Duke bow;
A fervent friendship sends he, greeting,
And in humility.
Through his Embassador, our Grand Duke begs
To know the pleasure of great France
Regarding Tuscany.

BONAPARTE.

Signor Marquis ;
Of that rare creditor you do remind me
Who once did importune in modest phrase,
Coupled with flattery and confidence,
The Cardinal de Rohan when he would
Be "kind enough" to pay him.   "My dear Sir,"
Said the Cardinal, "I pray you do not be
So very curious."

(*Turns to Caulaincourt.*)

I am tired of this jugglery !

CAULAINCOURT.

The Ambassadors of Venice wait without.

BONAPARTE.

(*Furiously.*)

If they the treasures of Peru should proffer me
'Twould not atone the blood their treachery
Has cost my soldiers !
My soldiers are my children—they have murdered them !
The Lion of St. Mark must lick the dust !
Say that to Venice I will be an Attila !

Enter Mme. De Stael.)

JOSEPHINE.

(*Approaching De Stael.*)

Madame !

(*She leads her to Bonaparte.*)

(*To Bonaparte.*)

You have not forgotten our great friend !

DE STAEL.   (*Aside.*)

Clever !

BONAPARTE.

Not while I remember France.

DE STAEL.

Ah, General, you do exalt me !

BONAPARTE.

Genius itself does nominate.

DE STAEL.

Among the ancients was this true, indeed,
And virtue was permitted to take rank.
To seek the plaudits, the esteem of Rome
Was reckoned worthy of ambition ;
But now when one may glide by stealth to glory
All powerful is mediocrity.

BONAPARTE.

Patience, Madame, since to the truly great
Death lends the grand perspective.

DE STAEL.

And still we make our own comparisons.
Now, tell me, General, whom should you name
The greatest of all women in fair France ?

BONAPARTE.

The mother who has nobly borne to France
Her sons.

DE STAEL.

Like England's famous King,
'Twould seem that you lack soldiers.

(*Laughing.*)

BONAPARTE.

What France lacks most is virtuous, true womanhood.
Let me turn questioner.   What seek you, then,
With your great talents and pre-eminence?

DE STAEL.

The companionship of genius you deny me—
The official muse of your great Iliad.

BONAPARTE.

In raising you to the high dignity
Of my antagonist, I have aggrandized you.

DE STAEL.

Ah, yes, a cruel fate you give to me—
I shall have a few lines in your history!

BONAPARTE.

But not as my Delilah ! Nor yet shall you,
As Egypt's queen, have place on history's page
Because you wrecked the soldier
Of our Modern Rome.

> (*Enter an officer of Chasseurs.
> He goes to Bonaparte gives dis-
> patch and exits.   Bonaparte
> reads the dispatch.*)

DE STAEL.   (*Aside.*)

I have met but one great man, ruler of souls,
And he is the one tyrant of my life.
I do regret I spoke so bitterly—
But why should I repent?   What matters it?
I who may have a nation at my feet,

Princes for slaves, and kings at my command !
Can he despise me ?
What though I did offend him ?   It is nothing—
Nothing—he cannot quite ignore me—
What, then, and if he should ?   What matters it ?
And if he should ?   What strange emotion this ?
My heart stands still—Ignore me !

> (*During the speech of De Stael,
> Bonaparte has hurriedly read
> the dispatch, writes and, at the
> conclusion of her aside, ap-
> proaches her.*)

BONAPARTE.

(*To De Stael.*)

Madame, France owes you much.   You will be pleased
To increase her obligations.   This paper
Contains instructions to that end, Madame.
We have made you our Ambassador.

> (*He hands her the paper
> and passes to Josephine.*)

DE STAEL.

> (*Reads, aside.*)

" *Mme. De Stael :*

My information warrants your immediate arrest.
It is my desire to save you from humiliation.   Be
pleased, Madame, to withdraw at once.   You will find
an officer in attendance at your carriage who will conduct you beyond the lines of my army.   Your future
safety will lie outside of the confines of France.

BONAPARTE."

(*To Bonaparte.*)

Your embassage is weighty, yet will I bear it.
I take my honored leave and shall report
Right speedily.   (*Exit De Stael.*)

JOSEPHINE.

(Aside to Bonaparte.)

I fear, love, you have erred.

BONAPARTE.

A paltry error—
Well, what matters it?

JOSEPHINE.

At worst, what was she but a gossiper?

BONAPARTE.

Twixt gossip and intrigue there's fellowship
Doth make blood brotherhood.

JOSEPHINE.

A woman's eyes best see a woman's heart—
She loved you and opposing you but sought
First to command attention by her wit,
Then your respect by her great cleverness,
Your admiration by audacity.
Building on these with all the subtle charms
The brilliant genius of a woman may
She hoped to win, but did not seek to wrong.

BONAPARTE.

Such creatures are incapable of love.

(Enter the Princess Augusta.)

AUGUSTA.

Are all friends?

*(Josephine rings. Enter a page
who closes curtain between first
and second rooms.)*

BONAPARTE.

All.

AUGUSTA.

Base villainy and black ingratitude !

BONAPARTE.

Well—

AUGUSTA.

The plot was deeper laid than did appear,
Completer in detail and the award
Offered alike for capture or assassination.
Botot is superseded and tells all.

BONAPARTE.

Well—well—How far have they progressed ?

AUGUSTA.

Not yet so far, thanks to Monsieur Botot,
Or, rather, to his weakness, but they may
Be easy ta'en in it.   Here is a list
Of the conspirators.

> (*Hands the list to Bona-
> parte. He looks it over.*)

BONAPARTE.

So—So!— My enterprising friends ! So—So !

JOSEPHINE.

We did succeed in sending the dispatch—

AUGUSTA.

Your messenger was apprehended.

BONAPARTE.

No time must now be lost—

(*To Augusta.*)

Return to Paris and resume your part.
Require a meeting of these same conspirators.
How long will't take you to accomplish it?

AUGUSTA.

From my arrival?

BONAPARTE.

Yes.

AUGUSTA.

Four and twenty hours.

BONAPARTE.

You have Barras well in hand.

AUGUSTA.

I hold the reins.

BONAPARTE.

There's magic in a pretty woman's smile.

AUGUSTA.

More power
In her will.

BONAPARTE.

Wear both to their full potency.
Reach Paris on the fifth—upon the sixth
Bring them together, say at eight 'o the evening.
Command your own attendance—

(*Exit Augusta.*)

(To Murat.)

Prepare you for our journey, General :
In four and twenty hours we shall follow—
Our work must rest here·till we may return—
Thus are our brightest hopes oft made to wait
Upon the snail-paced tread of destiny.

(Rings. Enter a page.)

My Secretaries !   *(Exit page.)*

(Enter three Secretaries.)

(They sit at separate tables.)

(To First Secretary.)

Citizen Directory :

I owe you an open confession.   My heart is depressed and filled with horror through the attacks of the Parisian journals.

(To Second Secretary.)

General Moreau :

Arrest at once Monsieur Botot and send him to these headquarters.

(To Third Secretary.)

General Joubert :

Your presence is requested at these headquarters.

(To First Secretary.)

I am "keeping the plunder" whilst I am defeating them.   I "affect despotism" whilst I speak only as General-in-Chief; I "assume Supreme power" and yet submit to law.   Everything I do is·turned to crime against me.   The poison streams over me.

(To Second Secretary.)

Let him be attended closely, but let no violence nor insult be offered him.

(To First Secretary.)

Were any one in Italy to dare give utterance to the thousandth part of these calumnies I would impose upon him an awful silence.

(To Third Secretary.)

Travel in all possible haste.

(To First Secretary.)

In Paris this is allowed to go on unpunished and your tolerance is an encouragement. The Directory is thus producing the impression that it is opposed to me. If the Directors suspect me, let them say so and I will justify myself. If they are convinced of my uprightness, let them defend me.

(To Second Secretary.)

Treat him, indeed, right civilly.

(To First Secretary.)

In this circle of argument I include the Directory with me, and cannot go beyond it. My desire is to be useful to my country; must I, for reward, drink the cup of poison?

(To Second Secretary.)

General Moreau :

Arrest at once and hold in close confinement the friend of Botot, who recently arrived with him from France, wearing a colonel's uniform.

(To Josephine.)

Of infantry ?

JOSEPHINE.

Of infantry.

BONAPARTE.

(To Second Secretary.)

Of infantry.

(To First Secretary.)

I can no longer be satisfied with empty, evasive arguments; and if justice is not done to me I must *take* it myself.

(To Third Secretary.)

General Marmont:

Arrest at once the Abbe Sergi, and send to these headquarters.

(To Second Secretary.)

General Moreau:

Let no movement of General Pichegrue be unknown to you. He is plotting with the Bourbons.

(To First Secretary.)

Therefore, I am yours. Salutation and brotherly love.

(Bonaparte hastily signs the dispatches.)

(To Caulaincourt.)

See that these dispatches are sent at once.

(Turning to his Generals.)

This artifice
That instigates employment of assassins—

(Enter a page. Curtains between first and second rooms drawn back.)

PAGE.

The Count Von Coblentz from the Court of Austria.

BONAPARTE.

Admit him!

(*Sensation.*)

Never was reptile, neath a conqueror's foot
Could wriggle like the Austrian !
The time has come to crush !

(*Enter the Count Von Coblentz.*)

(*To Coblentz.*)

Now, now, another embassy ?
I am tired of this vacillation
Heartily ! In fourteen days *thus* will I dash
The Austrian Monarchy to pieces !

(*As he speaks the word " thus"*
he seizes a vase* from the man-
tel and dashes it to the floor.)

(*To Caulaincourt.*)

Say to the Archduke Charles,
In the name of General Bonaparte,
The truce is at an end.

COBLENTZ.

Mercy ! Mercy !

BONAPARTE.

Ah !—Is Austria at my feet ?
There may she rest in peace !

TABLEAU.

---

* This vase was of rare value—a gift of The Empress Catharine.

MME. DE STAEL.

ACT IV.—SCENE FIRST.

PARIS.

PARLORS OF MME. BONAPARTE.

Discovered -
Barras and the Princess Augusta.

BARRAS

BUT tell me now, Sweet, why this present haste?
Will not to-morrow, or the next day, or—

AUGUSTA.

The next, or next—within a week, perhaps,
Or surely by the month's end! Is it thus
You would evince your overpowering love,
That all consuming flame you've fanned so oft
By blowing of your eloquence upon't?
Would heaven I were a man!

BARRAS.

An' if you were, my love?

AUGUSTA.

I'd be a man!
A man contented not with woman's love,
But only with her worship, as, indeed,
She'd look up to a demi-god!

BARRAS.

Now, Sweet! My little Sweet!

AUGUSTA.

Sweet me no sweets!
You are only sweet in promises.

BARRAS.

But should I promise to the end you seek?

AUGUSTA.

Oh, will you?

BARRAS.

And if I should?

AUGUSTA.

And keep it?

BARRAS.

If you then doubt me, wherefore should I promise!

AUGUSTA.

I will not doubt you—only promise me!

BARRAS.

Then—Then—I promise.

AUGUSTA.

Then you'll meet to-night?

BARRAS.

To-night.

AUGUSTA.

At eight, say you?

BARRAS.

Even at eight—
Though 'tis an early hour.

AUGUSTA.

I can scarce wait for't—
If I have seemed impatient for this meeting,
Pardon me! I am impetuous for thee
To seize what is thine own ; am selfish
And I own it. I would be near to thee
Continually, but cannot be till this,
Thy right, is once established. Bear with me
If I seem over fond! Thou must rule France!

BARRAS.

Bear with thee? "Bear," saidst thou? Now, by my faith,
I'd bear thee to earth's end!

(*Offers to embrace her.*)

AUGUSTA.

Soft, you, my love!
Bear, also, a becoming modesty!
The hour passes—waste no time, I pray.
Between this and our happy wedding day.

BARRAS.

All lovers have some time for dalliance.

AUGUSTA.

Are we, then, of the herd? Learn patience, sir.

BARRAS.

Must I then go?

AUGUSTA.

At once.

BARRAS.

Ah, my sweet love!

(*Exit Barras.*)

AUGUSTA.

Now for my page suit—then to follow him.
If Bonaparte meet no delay—Ah! Ah!
Well, I have played the Count down to the hour,
So much for will, and one weak woman's power.

ACT IV.—SCENE SECOND.

PARLORS OF HOTEL ELBOEF.

(Enter Bonaparte and Murat.)

BONAPARTE.

IT is upon the hour.

MURAT.

The Princess will not fail?

BONAPARTE.

Fail!
Had she skill at arms she has of wit
I'd give her command of my guard.
Brave as thou art, thou may'st learn courage of her ;
True as thou art, she'll teach to thee devotion.

(Enter Augusta disguised as a page.)

Well, boy, who bade?—Ha, 'tis a fair disguise !

AUGUSTA.

Soft, you !   They're but a wall away.
You are well upon the hour.

BONAPARTE.

An hour, a single moment, late, may lose
An army.   I said I should be here.

AUGUSTA.

I said *they* should be here.

BONAPARTE.

Murat, what think you of her mettle now?

AUGUSTA.

This key unlocks the door of the drawing room.

> (*Gives key to Bonaparte.*)

Here shall you wait their coming. They'll be here
Presently.

> (*Shows Bonaparte and Murat into
> room, then listens at door.*)

They think this parlor vacant.
You'll hear their conversation readily—
The attendants are all mine. An' you command,
You'll find them trusty. So, God be with you!

> (*She closes door and exits.*)
> (*Enter Barras, Gohier, Moulins
> and five other Conspirators.*)

BARRAS.

> (*Continuing his speech.*)

S'death! They did squander gold on Serbelloni!
Made it a rival for the Tuileries!
All Italy
And the nobility of Lombardy
Vied with each other who should humblest be.
Then follows Montebello in the train,
Seeking to overtop all rivalry,
And Venice to appease him makes his spouse
A veritable queen. Jove, what magnificence!
Now have we dallied long enough in this—

GOHIER.

What says the General, Pichegrue,
Touching Moreau?

BARRAS.

He finds him more ready
Than pliable.

GOHIER.

Well, well, unfold!

BARRAS.

Moreau
Is for Moreau.

GOHIER.

What! Stands he not with us?

BARRAS.

Only so far as we shall favors grant
Monsieur Moreau.   In his own looking glass,
Fondly presuming that it is the world,
He gazes steadily, and cannot comprehend
Why the great central figure stands not out
In bold relief to others as to himself.
Another meeting is appointed now
With Georges at his safe retreat, Chaillot.
But poor Rivier is driven to despair
And talks but of the apathy of France.

GOHIER.

He lacks in courage and tenacity.
Were't not for Mme. Bonaparte I'd chance
A fortune on our quick success.
She has all the eyes of Paris after us,
And for herself I think she never sleeps.

BARRAS.

Ere this the Corsican's a corpse, or else
A prisoner. Either event demands
We make swift preparation for the news—
First to appease the people—

MOULINS.

But the army?

BARRAS.

To Pichegrue—

(Enter Bonaparte and Murat.)
(Sensation.)

BONAPARTE.

How now? Have we surprised you, gentlemen?

BARRAS.

You honor us, General—

GOHIER.

Yes.

MOULINS.   `

Yes.

BONAPARTE.

You seem confused!

BARRAS.

You come quite unannounced—

BONAPARTE.

It would appear so.

BARRAS.

But you are not
The less welcome.

GOHIER.

No, none the less welcome—

MOULINS.

Oh, you are very, very welcome—

BONAPARTE.

Peace!
Can it be possible!   Murat, look you
Upon these men! For we will call them men—
Duplicity ne'er had a throne till now.
Oh, precious knaves! Was ever innocence
Protected by more placid mien?

BARRAS.

Beware! The voice of the Directory,
The great Directory of France, now rests
In those you would accuse! Look well to it!

BONAPARTE.

What! Threat you us before our very face?
Why, here is now assurance worth a cause!
"Beware!" Oh, most refreshing!
"Beware!" Why, now, Murat, this is sublime!
When, 'neath the shadows of the Pyramids,
We'll have this to inspire us, this "Beware!"

(*Barras and conspirators
draw.   Murat draws.*)

BARRAS.

Have at them ! Let us finish here.

(*They rush upon Bonaparte, Murat advances to meet them. Bonaparte* LOOKS *upon them and they fall back.*)

BONAPARTE.

(*To Murat.*)

When did you fall so low
That you would put yourself 'gainst carrion ?
Austria would refuse to cross your sword
Wearing such blood upon it !

Hear me, now,

(*To Conspirators.*)

You miserable hangers on of time !
You would-be arch-conspirators,
But that you lack both wit and valor for it ;
I will not send you to the guillotine—
You are too base; to exile, for there's not
A land I'd curse with you ; nor yet to dungeons !
No, you shall live, as other monstrous things,
But, unlike them, you shall dwell in the light.
As they would prosper in a noisome cell
So shall you not, feeding on martyrdom ;
As they would blister in the noontide sun
So shall you blister in the glare of honesty
Till, when through every maddening memory,
Remorse shall sting you to the soul's quick core,
Unknown, not e'en dispised, each one of you
Shall crawl in his own slime down to oblivion !
Begone !

(*Exit conspirators, Bonaparte regarding them.*)

MURAT.

I had enjoyed some pastime with the dogs

BONAPARTE.

The hydra had not felt the loss.　These heads
Were quick replaced.　We'll strike the monster's heart!
That's England !

MURAT.

But are these powerless?

BONAPARTE.

No.　And yet less powerful than those
Who would take their places.　Even these
Have the ear of the people.　This act will prompt
To rashness, then the people are with us.
The Army's ours already !

ACT IV.—SCENE THIRD.

A STREET IN PARIS.

NIGHT.

Discovered—

Barras and Gohier.

BARRAS.

IS all ready?

GOHIER.

Waiting for his coming.

BARRAS.

Then shall we see
If now his "Goddess" will protect him.
Carbon and St Rejeant, are they still firm?

GOHIER.

I have reserved the sum we promised them.

BARRAS.

Who will apply the torch?

GOHIER.

St. Rejeant's self.

BARRAS.

The Place?

GOHIER.

The Rue St. Nicaise.

BARRAS.

Can they fail?

GOHIER.

Impossible!
Carbon and Limoelan will watch
The progress of the Consul's carriage,
As it shall leave the Tuileries,
Till time to give the signal to St. Rejeant.

BARRAS.

Let us be gone—the time approaches—
We must not be seen.

(*Exeunt.*)

(*As they go off a rumbling noise is heard, followed by the appearance of the guard and carriage of Bonaparte. The scene changes to the Rue St. Nicaise where a cart is discovered with infernal machine in it, a little girl holding the horse and St. Rejeant off at one side. The carriage passes, after which there is an explosion, destroying cart and child. Scene changes back, when the consul's carriage is discovered passing safely.*)

(*Re-enter Barras and Gohier.*)

GOHIER.

He did escape us!

BARRAS.

But all hell's power shall not save him.

GOHIER.

We'll find no time for napping from this time out.

BARRAS.

Then to your wits.

GOHIER.

I tremble so
I don't collect my wits.

BARRAS.

S'death! Man!
Only the boldest front can serve us now.

GOHIER.

A fellow must be brave to look it well.

BARRAS.

Join me to-morrow in the council—
Bring all your stock of courage, for you may
Have need of it.

GOHIER.

How now?

BARRAS.

How now? How now? Why, damn it, nothing now!
But then! Then! Then!—By hell, I swear, that then
In presence of them all I will arraign him
For high treason! Come, let us mature it—
'Tis a bold venture.

ACT IV.—SCENE FOURTH.

ANTE-ROOM OF THE COUNCIL CHAMBER.

Discovered—

> Bonaparte, Caulaincourt, Eugene, Murat, Lannes,
> Lefebre and Devoust.

BONAPARTE.

(Continuing his speech.

AND thus is stands;
  When the Republic trembled in the grasp
  Of the combined strength of all the thrones,
Then rushed we to the rescue and our arms
Did win the grandest victories of time.
From anarchy the Constitution rose
And spread its ample wings o'er our beloved France.
A god-like impulse sent us then to Egypt
In the noblest enterprise and most magnificent
Man for his fellowmen has e'er conceived.
Had we then won, we had knocked off the chains
Of Asia's countless millions.   From slavery
The basest, cruelest, we had lifted them
To all the glorious possibilities
Of intellectual, enlightened freedom ;
Made of them men, infused with energy,
Assisted them to the development
Of all that Science, Art and noble purpose
Could wrest from inexhaustible resource.
We had builded such an empire in the orient
As Earth had never dreamed of.

In the midst of victories unparalleled
We were compelled to give o'er that great cause
To rescue France from parricides—
The Constitution's gone and Anarchy
Reigns everywhere.

MURAT.

Command us!

BONAPARTE.

Ah, gentlemen, what woeful sight is this!
Prosperity and Peace left we in France,
A name the synonym of martial glory.
We find her rent with strife, while wicked hands
Rifle her coffers and pollute her honor.
Creatures of foreign states sit in her councils,
The very air is pestilent with treason!
We must strike, or all is lost.

(*Enter a Courier.*)

COURIER.

The Council's in a tumult.

(*Exit Courier.*)

BONAPARTE.

Gentlemen, we will end it!

(*Exeunt.*)

ACT IV.—SCENE FIFTH.

THE COUNCIL OF THE FIVE HUNDRED.

LUCIEN BONAPARTE, Presiding

(Confusion.)

GOHIER.

THEN let me in conclusion urge
A new election. The fate of France,
No less, depends upon it.

FIRST MEMBER.

No! No! No!
Such haste shows base cowardice!

SECOND MEMBER.

Shame! Shame!
(Cheers on the right.)

THIRD MEMBER.

Such language is an insult to the council!
(Cheers on the left.)

THE PRESIDENT.

This strife must cease! 'Twill end in anarchy!

GOHIER.

I rise to ask the member if his charge
Of cowardice means to apply to men
Or measures?

FIRST MEMBER.

To both !

GOHIER.

Then I hurl it back and challenge to a test !

(*Great confusion.*)

BARRAS.

This is madness ! Are we devoid of reason ?
Who is to profit by this senseless strife ?
The great Republic ?   No ! Nor you, nor I,
Nor either of our factions ! Who seeks
The good of France ?

FIRST MEMBER.

Not Barras.

THIRD MEMBER.

Bah ! Bah ! Bah !

FIRST MEMBER.

Conspirator ! Behold the arch-conspirator !

VOICES.

Conspirator ! Conspirator !

BARRAS.

I ask again—

FIRST MEMBER.

Show us your purse of English Gold !

SECOND MEMBER.

Treason ! Treason !

BARRAS.

Are ye not Frenchmen?   I ask again :
Who seeks the good of France?   Then let him, now,
Propose a sacrifice that he will make,
And I will clasp his hand and go with him.
What, then, are we, through passion, to lose all?
In this extremity shall we invite
Foul anarchy?   The usurper comes
By stealthy strides—Even now is at our gates.

(*Enter Bonaparte and Murat.*)

Behold ! At the very word he comes !
Away with him !

THIRD MEMBER.

Down with him !

ANOTHER MEMBER.

He is a traitor !

ANOTHER MEMBER.

Cromwell !

A MULTITUDE OF VOICES.

Down with the usurper !

(*Wild confusion.*)

BONAPARTE.

Citizens ! Hear me !

VOICES.

Down with him ! Traitor ! Traitor ! Usurper !

BONAPARTE.

Will you not hear me?

VOICES.

No! No! Down with him!

(*They draw and rush upon him. Members rise, shouting and gesticulating wildly. The conspirators crowd around Bonaparte threateningly.*)

BONAPARTE.

Back, slaves! Within this form throbs the quick heart
Of France, protected by the awful power
Of the assembled worlds! Lo, in these hands
I grasp the thunderbolts of Fate!

(*They fall back. Murat signals the grenadiers at the door and they surround Bonaparte.*)

VOICES.

Down with the usurper! He brings soldiers
To overawe us.

BONAPARTE.

Who loves me, let him follow me!

(*He advances to the President's chair. The conspirators make a show of violence, but are quickly discovered.*)

Arrest the conspirators,
In the name of France and Bonaparte!

(*Barras, Gohier, Moulins, Second and Third Members and others are surrounded by the grenadiers.*)

So, gentlemen, at last you measure strength with me !
Away with them !

(*Exeunt grenadiers and prisoners.*)

Goddess above all I thank thee !
Sweet France, now will I give thee power
Shall grasp the globe ! Starred with thy vassal states
Thy canopy shall measure glory
With the dome of worlds !

CURTAIN.

•

ACT V.—SCENE FIRST.

AN ANTE-ROOM OF NOTRE DAME.

(Enter * Bonaparte, Caulaincourt, Eugene, Murat, Lannes, and Ney.)

BONAPARTE.

THUS, though we foes destroy without, within
Still for our loved Republic, there's no peace ;
The Powers still plot our overthrow.

MURAT.

Vive l'Armee!

BONAPARTE.

Shall we, then, fight interminably ?
Are men created but for slaughter ?   Pah !
What boots it though we vanquish, o'er and o'er,
The Allied Powers, their creatures in our midst ?
We are already weary of our victories.
What, though, from Chaos we should build again
The Constitution and the outward forms
Proclaiming the Republic ?   Is't stronger
Than the Consulate ?   Nay, nor yet weaker ;

---

* "Bonaparte was magnificently attired in a costume after the style of the XVI Century, designed by the greatest painter of his day. He wore a plumed hat and short mantle and did not assume the Imperial costume until the Coronation Ceremony."
—Thiers.

Each to the world is equal in offense.
France must needs have fair peace and such employ
As shall give life to the Industries and Arts
And Science and Philosophy.
Give us ten years of peace and our advance
Will astound the world more than our victories.

CAULAINCOURT.

Peace? Is it then possible?

BONAPARTE.

The Powers war not against France, but the Republic,
The Consulate, or any form, save Monarchy.
We'll rob them of all pretense of offense!
Fate wills—We do but execute.

(*Exeunt.*)

ACT V.—Scene Second.

NOTRE DAME.

The Coronation.

Pantomime.

UPON the opening of this scene is discovered the interior of Notre Dame, decorated with unequaled magnificence. The throne of the Emperor and Empress represents a sort of monument within a monument between two columns, supporting a pediment upon which is a representation of the Crown of Charlemagne.

On the left is seen the throne designed for the Pope, over which is a pediment supporting a diamond cross.

Directly in front of either throne, and in the centre of the stage, is the Altar, on which are seen the Imperial Robes, the Sword, the Scepter and the Imperial Crowns.

Enter Pope Pius VII.,

Preceded by the Cross and attended by the Sixty Prelates of the French Church, as the musicians chant the "*Tu es Petrus.*" He kneels at the altar and then ascends his throne.

The Prelates approach, salute him and arrange themselves on his right and left.

Enter * Napoleon and Josephine,

Attended by the Bonaparte family, Eugene, Augusta, and maids of honor, Generals and high dignitaries.

Napoleon and Josephine approach the altar and kneel.

---

* "At this stage of the ceremony Napoleon wore only the crown of the Cæsars, namely, a simple golden laurel. All admired that noble head, noble beneath that golden laurel as some antique medallion."

—Thiers.

THE POPE

Descends from his throne and comes to the altar, lifting his hands over them in blessing.

NAPOLEON

Raises his head and is anointed by the Pope on forehead, arms and hands.

THE POPE

Takes the sword and blesses it and, as Napoleon rises, girds it upon him.

The Pope then offers to take up the crown, but Napoleon suddenly reaches it himself and deliberately places it upon his own head. He then takes the crown of the Empress and, as she is still kneeling at his feet, places it with visible tenderness upon her head. Taking her by the hand, she arises.

THE POPE

Blesses the Scepter and places it in the hand of Napoleon.

THE EMPEROR AND EMPRESS

Are invested in the Imperial Robes and ascend their throne.

THE ARCH-CHANCELLOR

Approaches the throne and, presenting a Bible, Napoleon reverently places his hand upon it.

THE POPE

chanting the "*Vival in æternum semper Augustus*" of Charlemagne, advances to the throne, lifting his hands in benediction.

CHANT OF THE PONTIFICIAL HIGH MASS.

CANNON AND BELLS WITHOUT.

TABLEAU.

ACT V.—SCENE THIRD.

THE IMPERIAL PALACE.

EMPEROR'S CABINET.

NIGHT.

Napoleon Discovered.

NAPOLEON.

THUS far hath Fate fulfilled her covenant—
    From conquest on to conquest hath She led me.
    'Till now my Sceptered power, invincible,
With glory crowns a greater France—My France !
  But at what price ? What sighs ! What tears !
What anguish ! What despair ! What soul-defeat !
The wailing of a Continent is heard—
The cost of the Empire—The price of Peace !
  And soon shall come, even for Thy son,
Oh, Fate, the end decreed for all ! And then ?
On whom shall the Imperial Mantle rest ?
Childless, thou leavest me to reign alone !
Across the abyss of death, no hand can reach
To sustain the Throne of France !
  Do they, the jealous and malignant Gods,
Combine 'gainst us ? O'er Thee may none prevail !
Bear, then, oh, Goddess, swift as His lightnings,
Even to the great throne of the Thunderer,
Defiance !

So let our bond become inseparable—
Subdue the Immortals, thou, the earth
Leave unto me!
Now will I bridge the chasm over death—
An heir born in The Purple must take up
My work, whose hand shall still sustain thy throne,
Dear France! Aye! Though it cost me Josephine!

(Enter Josephine.)

Josephine!—My peerless one!

JOSEPHINE.

Did'st call me love?   Wherefore with voice so wild,
So sorrowful?

NAPOLEON.

Oh, do not leave me!

JOSEPHINE.

My noble one! Knowest thou not my love?

NAPOLEON.

Thou must not go!

JOSEPHINE.

Are we not one?
What power could separate us?   Oh, my own!
Upon that altar touched by God's right hand,
Love kindled into flame a holy fire
Has melted into oneness our two souls!
There is no power can separate us now!

NAPOLEON.

Would that it had consumed my mortal part
And but a trace remained, a throb, a thought,

Whatever form a soul is purest in,
That it might now be buried in thy soul
And find its heaven there eternally !

JOSEPHINE.

Oh, my dear love !

NAPOLEON.

Men call me great,
And yet if they did know what greatness costs !
He may not know who has not paid the price !

JOSEPHINE.

Dear love, am I so much to thee ?

NAPOLEON.

Thou art to me the epitome of life—
There is no God if love be not His breath !

JOSEPHINE.

Confess I dare not all thou art to me—
I fear—I fear that I do worship thee !

NAPOLEON.

Oh, France ! France ! France ! Now dost thou ask too much!

JOSEPHINE.

Nay, come ! Thou must be strong ! My dear, dear love !

(*Exeunt.*)

ACT V.—Scene Fourth.

Drawing Room of the Empress.

(Enter Eugene and Augusta.)

EUGENE.

AND this—and this is greatness!

AUGUSTA.

Ah! Yes.   But are we the happier?

EUGENE.

No! Let us confess it, no, Augusta!
In the attaining, not in the thing attained,
Our happinesses come.   The souls unrest
Cannot be satisfied.

AUGUSTA.

But we have reached
A careful height, so let us bask, Love,
In our little glory.—Why do you sigh?

EUGENE.

My sigh was for the Empress, not her son.

AUGUSTA.

What!   Has the Emperor declared himself?

EUGENE.

No, not in words.

AUGUSTA.

By act, then?   Tell me all!

EUGENE.

I left my mother a short hour ago;
She had sent for me and when I met her,
Fell upon my neck and, weeping bitterly,
Told me she could no longer hope—bade me
Try, with her, to feel that this great sacrifice
Was but her part for France.

AUGUSTA.

Has he, then, signified his purpose?

EUGENE.

She but infers it from his manner.

AUGUSTA.

Ah! yes, I see—He is overfond,
Demonstrative.   Caresses her
As though 'twere but a little day preceding
A long absence, and in an hundred ways
Betrays himself.   Alas! Poor Empress!

EUGENE.

This interview and my unhappy dream
Have left me almost fitted for despair.

AUGUSTA.

A dream?   An unhappy dream?

EUGENE.

Last night I dreamed our Paris was besieged ;
I, second in command, had been to inspect
The outposts.   The night wore on towards morning,
When a sound as of the distant roaring
Of artillery, drew my attention
To the South and East—The cloudless heavens
Were glorious with stars—Louder, deeper
The terrible reverberation rolled,
Nearer, until the very dome of heaven
Seemed to tremble.   Then, through the vaulted azure
Rushed chariots of war, drawn by fierce steeds
Whose dilate nostrils sent forth lightnings,
Until the sun from out a sea of blood
Leaped forth a world of fire !
The Emperor, with folded arms, the while,
Strode to and fro upon the parapet,
Regarding silently.   But as the sun
Came forth, he stumbled, fell,
Without the battlements.

AUGUSTA.

Nay, Dear, be not cast down !

EUGENE.

I can no longer bear this hateful masque !
If Love and Power may not go hand in hand
Then farewell Power ! I'll seek obscurity.
Oh, let us flee this miserable place
Before our loves become contaminate
With the infection of these heavy hours !
Put thy dear hand in mine, my precious wife ;
And with our grief-bowed mother we will seek
That richest prize of earth, Contentment,
With Love and Peace and all the blessed saints
That cluster round the hearthstone of a home.

AUGUSTA.

Ah ! Do not tempt me from my destiny !
My woman's heart pleads but to obey,
Aye, happily anticipate obedience !
You know I love you, dearer than my life ;
But shall we now forsake the Emperor,
When most he needs us ?   The Emperor is France !

EUGENE.

Then you will not go with us ?

AUGUSTA.

Oh, Eugene !
I pray you do not put me to a test
Twixt Love and Duty !

EUGENE.

Your duty's to your love.

AUGUSTA.

Not when my love counsels against my duty.

(*Exeunt.*)

ACT V.—SCENE FIFTH.

EMPEROR'S CABINET.

Napoleon, discovered, asleep on a couch, Josephine sitting by him.

JOSEPHINE.

IN thy soft arms,
 Oh, hold him tenderly, sweet, gentle sleep !
 Hover above him, spirits of the blest,
On waves æolian, and touch his soul
With your divinest symphonies !
Let Lethe's spray in dewy showers fall
The while, may rays of hope shine through and show
A bow of promise on the heavy clouds
That now shut out our heaven !
                              Noble brow !
Realm of fair genius, throne of a lofty soul !
Ah, could I lift thy sorrows as I lift
These silken locks !
  Splendid orbs ! Where rests your glory now ?
Precious lips ! How oft my soul has melted
On you !

> (*Kisses him. She starts to go, but
> stops at exit and hears waking
> speech of Napoleon.*)
> (*Napoleon starts from his dream.*)

NAPOLEON.

Aye ! Aye ! 'Spite of the Immortal Gods !
Had every God the power of mighty Jove,

All leagued against my cause, yet will I hold
The scepter of Great France! My France!
'Tis I, Napoleon!

(Discovers Josephine.)

Ha! Josephine!
Why did'st thou leave me? Thou art my faith,
The safety of my soul!

JOSEPHINE.

Dear Love!

NAPOLEON.

Why, here are traces of thy tears—
Would I could weep!

JOSEPHINE.

Nay, I will weep for thee—
Thou must be strong!

NAPOLEON.

Strong? Teach me thy strength!

JOSEPHINE.

Dear God!

NAPOLEON.

Josephine, what is eternity?
Thou saidst, once, I should join thee there.

JOSEPHINE.

Yes—Yes—

NAPOLEON.

That we never should be separated there—

JOSEPHINE.

Yes—Yes—

NAPOLEON.

Are we not selfish, then, in this,
And weak of soul to grieve? A little while,
Only a little while and all is done.
A world awaits our action—
Look up! Look up! Or bid me curse myself!

> (*She looks up into his face. He
> gazes earnestly into hers, then em-
> braces her in great emotion, lays
> her upon the couch, regarding her
> as he goes off the stage.*)
> (*Josephine rises from couch.*)

JOSEPHINE.

Ah, siren Hope, no more! Else tune thy lyre
To a dirge! Sweet music is for those
Who live, or here, or on the other side,
But for the dying sing a requiem!
Ah, thy soft voice has touched my trusting heart
So oft that now the touch does wound where once
It had the power to heal! Peace! Away!—
Alone!
Last, only comfort, when the heart is crushed,
To be alone!— Come, now, my soul,
We will sit us down and nurse our loneliness.

> (*She sits on the floor.*)

Ah, Grief, thou art the only heir that I could bear!
I hold thee to my breast—Now feed and take
The life that gave thee life! Thou wast brought forth
In pain, thou givest pain in nursing,
Yet I hug thee close, for thou wast born of him.
My only treasure, thou, and thou'lt not depart—

And none will take thee from me—There's no one
Covets thee—Thou art welcome only here,
Here on thy mother's breast.
Ah, Grief, my babe, thy lips are cold,
Cold, cold thy form! Cold as dead love—
No, No! His love's not cold! He loves me!
    But, oh, he does not know how thou hast grown,
Feeding upon the currents of my life,
Until thou art so heavy—He does not know—
Ah! Ah! He shall not know!

(Rising.)

He is my world!
I cannot give him up! No! No! No!
Oh, my God!

(Going.)

Thou cling'st so close, my baby!
Nay, feed on! Where shall we go, my baby?
Feed on—Feed on—

*(She stops at the door observing the
entrance of Napoleon and starts
toward him, but checks herself,
remains and is then discovered by
Napoleon as indicated.)*

*(Re-enter Napoleon. He sits at
table, paper and writing material
before him. Shows great mental
distress and finally takes up pen to
write. The pen drops from his
hand.)*

NAPOLEON.

(Regarding his hand.)

Thou wouldst not tremble so
To sign my death warrant! Thou hast been firm,
Unfaltering, 'mid battle's din and roar,
And frightful cries of souls crushed out of men;
When to write one word, the voice of armies,

Spoke the doom of States—But one word, a name—
'Tis easy writ : Napoleon !

> (*Re-takes pen. Regards the drop of ink.*)

Eternity embraced within a drop !
Ah, little world, thou tremblest on a point !

> (*The drop of ink falls from the pen.*)

It has fallen ! My world is shattered !—
  Why, this is madness ! Am I then so weak ?
Is this Napoleon ?—
The hand that holds the destiny of France
Should bear a steadier nerve !
Thou hast shown thy loyalty to Josephine—
Now what thou owest to France !

> (*He writes.*)

'Tis done !

> (*As Napoleon says "'Tis done"
> and rises, the manuscript falls to
> the floor, the word DIVORCE is
> discovered written upon it. Jose-
> phine falls. Napoleon discovers
> her as he exclaims.*)

Now Fate, thou hag of hell, defy me !

CURTAIN.

FONTAINEBLEAU.

ACT VI.--SCENE FIRST.

PARLORS OF THE TUILERIES.

Discovered—

> Talleyrand, Molé, Cambaceries and Fouché.
> Augusta discovered at one side.

TALLEYRAND.

THIS silence bodes no good, I warrant you.

MOLE.

Pray you, how should it bode or good or ill?
Are we reduced to omens, gentlemen?

TALLEYRAND.

"Omens" or nothing an' you come to it.
The wilds of Russia, the incessant snows
And such protracted silence, all invite
Forebodings of disaster.

MOLE.

Well, then, I'll not
Accept the invitation.

CAMBACERIES.

Nor yet shall I.

FOUCHE.

Nor I.

TALLEYRAND.

I only trust you may not be compelled to.

FOUCHE.

The Emperor has, doubtless, got his hands full ;
What with the Russian and the early snows.
We'd pardon him to forget us for the while.

MOLE.

Your clemency will scarcely find occasion—

TALLEYRAND.

You think, then, 'tis from policy, alone,
His silence ?

MOLE.

Too oft has he been tried
To be judged otherwise.

FOUCHE.

Now is this true—
The General reigns on the battlefield
The while, in the affairs of state the Emperor.
I' the heat of the fight he sends commands to us
In every department of the state.

MOLE.

A day, or two, at most, will surely bring
Some tidings from him.

TALLEYRAND.

Surely we trust so.
But you that hope for glory in this war
Are hopefuller than I.

(Enter Metternich.)

METTERNICH.

Ah, gentlemen ! What news from Russia ?

TALLEYRAND.

None, none whatever—Not a single word !

METTERNICH.

'Twill come by doubles, presently.

MOLE.

Aye, freighted with a score of victories !

CAMBACERIES.

(To Fouche.)

Shall we go in to the banquet ?

(Exit Cambaceries and Fouche.)

TALLEYRAND.

(To Metternich.)

A word with you.

(Exit Talleyrand and Metternich.)

MOLE.

These two mean little good for us.

(Exit.)

ACT VI.—SCENE SECOND.

THE TUILERIES.

PRIVATE PARLORS OF THE EMPRESS.

MIDNIGHT.

(Enter the Princess Augusta and Maids.)

AUGUSTA.

THIS terrible suspense will quite outwear
The little strength that's left me !

FIRST MAID.

Dear Princess !
The Emperor's too great to be o'erthrown.

AUGUSTA.

Ah ! Ah ! A dark foreboding masters me—
A weight I may not lift burdens my soul !
Even while we speak the Emperor and Eugene,
Upon the cold earth in the wilds of Russia,
May both lie suffering or dead !

FIRST MAID.

Sweet Princess, do not lend yourself to grief!
You must have rest—

AUGUSTA.

Woo as I may, I cannot win repose.

(Confusion without.)

What can this mean?   Confusion in the Tuileries!

(Enter Napoleon in wraps.)

NAPOLEON.

Princess !

(Embraces her.)

AUGUSTA.

Why do you thus surprise us?   Are you well?

NAPOLEON.

We do surprise you quite against our will—
But all is well, else, indeed, were it not.
Yet, all's gone ill, Augusta—All's gone ill !

AUGUSTA.

All ?

NAPOLEON.

All—All—The army's gone !

AUGUSTA.

Where—Where—

NAPOLEON.

Whence it may not return—
. To the final glory that awaits
The soldier.

AUGUSTA.

But Eugene—Where is Eugene ?

NAPOLEON.

Eugene is spared to us and follows close—
How fares Josephine?

AUGUSTA.

Alas, poor lady!
Her heart is ever with you, and her tears
Have well nigh drained the fountain of her life.

NAPOLEON.

Ah! Ah! Poor Josephine! Alas! Alas!
She gave her life a willing sacrifice
And I, with my own hands, tore out her heart
And mine and laid them bleeding on the shrine
Of France!
But to what end?   That the hell hounds of Fate,
The damned hag, should lick the flames up
From that altar's crest, to follow hot
Upon my track forever after!
I pray you go—would I could go myself—
And tell her all—
Tell her that I am well and very strong;
For since my heart was sacrificed with hers
I have no heart to suffer—So commend me.

AUGUSTA.

(*To Second Maid.*)

I will set out at once—summon my escort.

(*Exit Maid.*)

NAPOLEON.

What of our Ministers?

AUGUSTA.

(*Giving Memorandum.*)

Therein you'll find, Sire, what I've noted.
I hope my fears wrong Talleyrand.

NAPOLEON.

The soul of a pure woman is oracular—
'Tis the defense that nature has provided.

(Glances over Memorandum.)

So—So—I had suspected him.
Three hours brings the dawn—I'll rest till then.
Please you have summoned all my ministers.

(Exit Augusta.)
(Napoleon throws himself on couch.)

ACT VI.—SCENE THIRD.

PARLORS OF THE TUILERIES.

Discovered—

> Talleyrand, Molé, Montalivet, Cambaceries, Fouché,
> and others.

———————

(Enter Napoleon, attended by
Caulaincourt, Duke of Vicenza.)

NAPOLEON.

I HAVE returned to you! The army rests—

TALLEYRAND.

Terrible!

NAPOLEON.

At best, we can but win what they have gained—
Shall we, then, grieve for our soldiers?

TALLEYRAND.

All's lost!

NAPOLEON.

Oh, no! We have our Talleyrand!

CAULAINCOURT.

We have, indeed, our Emperor!

NAPOLEON.

The army was invincible—Our march
To Moscow a continuous triumph!
As 'neath the sun of glorious Austerlitz
Melted the mighty legions of the Czar!
In twenty battles did we vanquish them
And drove them from their ancient capitol—
To resist us was impossible
To mortal power! But what mortals could not,
Could the elements—The Army's 'neath the snows!
Brave Caulaincourt shall tell you what remains—
He shall have leisure while we re-create
The army.

TALLEYRAND.

Do you still hope to win, Sire?

NAPOLEON.

Hope? No! The Emperor wills! To will's to do—
To do is but to will and it is done!
Impossible's a word he never knew.

(*To Montalivet.*)

Montalivet, what of the Interior?

MONTALIVET.

Your instructions, Sire, have been obeyed—
France never was more prosperous.

NAPOLEON.

Our Population?

MONTALIVET.

Is undiminished by the demands of war—
The past decade shows an increase.

NAPOLEON.

Our Industries?

MONTALIVET.

By your instructions, Sire, they have been advanced.

NAPOLEON.

Our Manufactures?

MONTALIVET.

Have prospered, Sire, beyond our greatest hopes.

NAPOLEON.

Our Agriculture?

MONTALIVET.

Our Agriculture is far in advance,
Greatly augmenting products of the soil ;
Cattle are multiplied, all breeds improved,
Horses and every useful animal.
Improvements, Sire, in all the useful Arts,
Experiments in every branch of labor,
And methods that have promised good results,
We have fostered, Sire, as thou didst direct.

NAPOLEON.

(*To Mole.*)

Count Molé, what of our Finance?

MOLE.

Your methods, Sire, make us inexhaustible.

NAPOLEON.

We have spent princely sums in the last decade !

MOLE.

And may spend princelier in the next decade.

NAPOLEON.

Your confidence reflects a zealous love.

MOLE.

My confidence is built upon my Emperor!

NAPOLEON.

> (*Speaking wholly from memory
> throughout this investigation.*)

Beyond what it has cost to defend ourselves against these enforced wars we have spent sixty-two million five hundred thousand francs on public buildings.

MOLE.

> (*Consulting memorandum in each
> of the answers that follow.*)

Yes, Sire.

NAPOLEON.

One hundred and twenty-five million francs on seaports, docks and harbors.

MOLE.

Yes, Sire.

NAPOLEON.

On roads and highways one hundred and seventy-five million francs.

MOLE.

Yes, Sire.

NAPOLEON.

On bridges in Paris and in the departments thirty-one million two hundred and fifty thousand francs.

MOLE.

Yes, Sire.

NAPOLEON.

On canals, embankments and drainage of lands, one hundred and twenty-five million francs.

MOLE.

You are two hundred thousand francs in error, Sire—a bagatelle compared with the general sum.

NAPOLEON.

One hundred million francs in public works in Paris.

MOLE.

Yes, Sire.

NAPOLEON.

And one hundred and fifty million francs on public buildings in the departments.

MOLE.

Yes, Sire.

NAPOLEON.

Why, 'tis almost a thousand million francs we have used in the improvements and embellishment of France !

MOLE.

* Sire ; if, from the age o' the Medici,
Or our own Louis Fourteenth, one could come
To gaze upon our marvelous achievements,
He'd ask : How many ages of fair peace
Did'st take to accomplish it?   The answer :
' Twelve years of war and but a single man.'

NAPOLEON.

Ah, gentlemen, matched 'gainst our fellow men
We may seem great—How puny is our strength
When set against the elements !

(*To Talleyrand.*)

Our Allies?

TALLEYRAND.

'Tis feared they waver, Sire.

NAPOLEON.

          Ah ! " 'Tis feared" they waver !
Do we not know?   Their friendship's but a masque
And has been given us grudgingly.
The crowned heads have made a common cause
Against France and against her Emperor,
Only to wait an opportunity.
Unmitigated hatred is their cause,
The force of arms alone will be their cure.

TALLEYRAND.

Are we sufficient, Sire, against the world?

---

* The words of Molé.

NAPOLEON.

And we are not, then must we surely fall!
For twelve long years we have but fought for peace
And, ever winning wondrous victories,
Have only asked an honorable peace.
Witness our first campaign in Italy,
Until at Campo Formio we forced
Most lenient terms upon an ungracious foe.
On our accession to the Consulate
We found the peace of Campo Formio broken.
How, then, we plead with England and with Austria—
With those who had so basely dealt with us!
    They spurned us and we promptly crossed the Alps
And met them on Marengo's bloody plain.
And on the field of that great victory
We sued for peace and only asked
The basis of the treaty they had broken.
    It was denied us and we promptly met
At Hohenlinden, and our glorious arms
Did triumph.   We had conquered peace,
The Peace of Amiens.
Prosperity now made her home in France ;
We grew to be the wonder of the world.
Again perfidious England broke her faith,
Her solemn covenant.   Great France was roused,
And by a unanimity of voice
Unprecedented in all history,
Proclaimed us Emperor.
    From our Imperial throne we plead for peace.
Their answer was the basest mockery
And a new coalition of the Powers.
Followed quick the wonderful campaign
Of Ulm and glorious Austerlitz,
And we forced peace on Austria.
    Another coalition took the field,
But our celerity and valorous arms

Soon mastered it.

To stop the flow of blood we plead for peace.
They would not hear our prayer and we,
Upon the fields of Jena and of Auerstadt,
Destroyed the Prussian Monarchy,
Then prayed for peace.   Their answer was
The infamous decree of England's King
Barring all commerce from the ports of France.

What, but retaliation, then was left ?
From Berlin and from Milan we replied.

Followed our great march to the Vistula
And then the frightful victory at Eylau.
Again we plead for peace, again repulsed
We marched to Friedland and the allied arms
Were utterly destroyed.   And we had conquered peace—
'Twas ratified at Tilsit.
Prosperity once more smiled on the Empire,
All other thrones were jealous of her smile.

Humanity now called our arms to Spain
And England sent her forces to oppose us,
Her emissaries to the Austrian Court,
And Austria armed.   How we did plead for peace !
But no avail.   Upon the gory field
Of Eckmuhl again we vanquished them,
Swept down the Danube with our glorious hosts,
Nor halted till their capitol was ours ;
Forced, then, the Danube and all earth amazed
By our achievements on the field of Wagram.
And again our arms had conquered peace—
The seventh coalition was o'erthrown.

Ah, gentlemen, had we been sterner there
And parcelled out the Austrian Monarchy !
My magnanimity has been my curse.

At Austerlitz I might have ta'en the Czar
And made my own terms with the Russian court ;
At Jena I had Prussia overthrown

And gave her back possession of her realm ;
At Wagram, Austria, only to restore
The life she had a fourth time forfeited.

CAULAINCOURT.

Posterity shall throne great Justice, Sire.

NAPOLEON.

And in the meantime, what is left but war?
You all do know we plead, aye, humbly plead,
We, who had nobly conquered half the world ;
Plead not as conquerors, but as suppliants,
To avert this war with Russia.
To supplication answered they with threats
And most unseemly insults.   What was their cause?
Base envy nurtured by perfidious courts,
Armed with the time-worn pretext that the Pole
Would one day give them trouble !   Commanded us
To break our plighted faith, give our consent
To that mild, harmless state's dismemberment !

TALLEYRAND.

But we are now without an army, Sire.

NAPOLEON.

Art thou an Austrian ?   What ! Know'st thou not
That every Frenchman is a soldier born?
A million soldiers wait but for my voice—
One word of mine will re-create the army !

*(Enter Marshal Ney,
in tattered uniform.)*

NEY.

Speak that one word and give me a command !

NAPOLEON.

(Embracing Ney.)

Glorious Ney! Thou bravest of the brave !
Oh, what a man wast thou ! What art thou now ?

NEY.

The rear-guard, Sire, of the grand army !
Upon the bridge of Kowno I did fire
Our last shot into the pursuing foe
Then threw my musket after it—Ha! Ha !
Give me a new command, Sire, and I'll fight
While there's a drop of red blood in my veins!

NAPOLEON.

My secretaries !
I'll call a million men—Our Veterans
Still number quite enough to marshal them.
Now shall we do such deeds 'neath sun and stars
Shall astound the Immortal Gods!

TABLEAU.

ACT VI.—SCENE FOURTH.

A STREET IN PARIS.

(Enter from either side citizens.)

FIRST CITIZEN.

VIVE l'Emperor !

SECOND CITIZEN.

Vive l'Emperor !

FIRST CITIZEN.

Can it be the Grand Army is overthrown ?

SECOND CITIZEN.

By the Russe, no ! By the snows, yes.

FIRST CITIZEN.

And the Emperor ?

SECOND CITIZEN.

As a wounded lion, roused now to a terrible effort !

FIRST CITIZEN.

Let them beware who are in his reach !

SECOND CITIZEN.

'Tis said the Austrian is plotting 'gainst us now.

FIRST CITIZEN.

Now? When did they not? Let the whole world plot!
Vive l'Emperor!

SECOND CITIZEN.

Vive l'Emperor!

ACT VI.—SCENE FIFTH.

A MILITARY ENCAMPMENT.

Discovered—

Marshals Ney, Eugene Beauharnais, Besseires, Soult, Duroc, Ouidinot, Macdonald, Mortier, Poniatowski and Davoust.

(Enter Napoleon and Caulaincourt.)

NAPOLEON.

COMRADES:
Before we march to this impending war
'Tis well you know what we shall have to meet,
Whom look to for support and all things else
Touching the weighty import of our cause—
I have no secrets from my soldiers.
The fair news first, good Caulaincourt,
'Tis easiest disposed of.

CAULAINCOURT.

We have addresses, Sire, innumerable
From our Parisian bodies and throughout
The confines of the Empire.
Besides, an hundred cities, Milan, Rome,
Florence, Turin, Hamburg, Amsterdam, Mayence.

NAPOLEON.

Read first from Milan.

CAULAINCOURT.

(Reading.)

"Our Kingdom, Sire, is your handiwork. It owes you its laws, its monuments, its roads, its property, its agriculture, the glory of its Arts and the internal peace which it enjoys. The people of Italy declare, in the face of the universe, that there is no sacrifice which they are not prepared to make to enable your Majesty to complete the great work intrusted to you by Providence.

In extraordinary circumstances, extraordinary sacrifices are required, and our efforts shall be boundless. All we possess, Sire, we lay at your Majesty's feet. This is not the suggestion of authority; it is conviction, gratitude, the universal cry produced by the passion for our political existence."

This, Sire, is a fair specimen of all the rest.

NAPOLEON.

Enough! You see that we have some friends left. Now of our enemies!

CAULAINCOURT.

England—

NAPOLEON.

The Pirate Queen of the northern seas!—Well?

CAULAINCOURT.

Has succeeded in forming another and stronger coalition.

NAPOLEON.

Well?

CAULAINCOURT.

To her own strength and that of Russia, Austria, renouncing her sacred treaty with France, has been added.

NAPOLEON.

Rather let us have declared enemies than doubtful allies. Well?

CAULAINCOURT.

Murat has abandoned the army and it is supposed will offer his services to the Coalition.

THE GENERALS.

Murat!

NAPOLEON.

A brave man on the battle field, but otherwise weak.

DAVOUST.

Murat is King not by the grace of God, but by the grace of your Majesty and the blood of French soldiers. He is inflated with base ingratitude.

NAPOLEON.

Poor Caroline! Well—Well?

CAULAINCOURT.

Our troops on the Spanish peninsula struggle against great odds—England, Portugal and Spain have combined a powerful army there.

NAPOLEON.

'Tis war to the death, my comrades, as you see.
A million Frenchmen answer to our call—
Three hundred thousand march with us tomorrow.
We will strike again for France!

ALL.

Vive, Vive l'Emperor! Vive La France!

NAPOLEON.

Upon our borders there already swarm
The Allied arms.   Is there a soldier now
Who would turn back, let him step forth!
Not one! Oh, Comrades, this is glorious!
This moves me more than victory.

NEY.

Bid us move forward, Sire, I cannot bear
To wait another hour!

NAPOLEON.

Forward the Old Guard! Forward!

———

ENTER THE OLD GUARD.

MARSHAL NEY TAKES COMMAND.

TABLEAU.

NAPOLEON

SURROUNDED BY HIS MARSHALS.

THE OLD GUARD PASSES IN REVIEW,

MARSHAL NEY IN COMMAND.

FRANCE, ADIEU.

ACT VII.—SCENE FIRST

ST. HELENA.

LONGWOOD.

(Enter two English officers in foreground.)

FIRST OFFICER.

WELL met, Comrade! How have you amused yourself?

SECOND OFFICER.

As usual. At dawn, witnessed the sunrise ; at eight, breakfasted ; from nine to twelve, our watch ; lunched at noon. Since which time I have been strolling over the island and am now going to dinner.

FIRST OFFICER.

I think this lazy life will end shortly.

SECOND OFFICER.

I trust so.

FIRST OFFICER.

If Bonaparte does not interfere by refusing to die.

SECOND OFFICER.

He fails fast.

FIRST OFFICER.

A shadow of glory.

SECOND OFFICER.

History will name him the greatest man of his age.

FIRST OFFICER.

History will do him justice.

SECOND OFFICER.

And England, too, and when it comes to speak of St. Helena, 'twill blot the English page.

FIRST OFFICER.

You speak boldly.

SECOND OFFICER.

As an Englishman should always speak who, proud of his country, scorns every act that reflects upon her honor.

FIRST OFFICER.

The Emperor—I mean Bonaparte, escaped from Elba.

SECOND OFFICER.

He was bound neither by law nor precedent to remain, and his reception by his countrymen forever silences the senseless cry of "Usurper."

FIRST OFFICER.

That was magnificent.

SECOND OFFICER.

Magnificent? It was glorious! Never, in all history, has anything approached it. A single man invades a nation, containing thirty million people, his friends gather about him, he marches seven hundred miles through the heart of the country to its powerful capitol, vanquishing, by his supreme presence, without the shedding of a drop of blood, the formidable armies sent to destroy him, and, in twenty days, is proclaimed Emperor amidst the greatest rejoicing and enthusiasm ever witnessed beneath the sun.

Ah, comrade, Bonaparte has ever been the Emperor of French hearts!

FIRST OFFICER.

My point was that, as he had escaped from Elba, we were justified in guarding him closely here.

SECOND OFFICER.

But Elba is not St. Helena. All the world knows that from this place escape is impossible, and the order that subjects the royal prisoner to the constant watching of English officers is inhuman.

FIRST OFFICER.

It is humiliating.

SECOND OFFICER.

To his proud spirit there could be nothing harder to bear, and this the authorities know.

FIRST OFFICER.

Now, if the truth were known, I think Sir Hudson, not our England, is at fault in this.

SECOND OFFICER.

Yet is Sir Hudson England, England Sir Hudson—So it
will be writ.

(Exeunt.)
*(Enter Napoleon, attended by Mar-
shal Bertrand and Marshand.)*

NAPOLEON.

And do you think they will attempt to enforce
These new indignities?

BERTRAND.

Yes, Sire, surely!

NAPOLEON.

What said this man, Sir Hudson, touching it?

BERTRAND.

That 'twas contended by the British Lords,
Of whom Lord Barthurst had addressed him,
That you were but a prisoner and as such
Should be treated—not with courtly honors.
Your titles being surrendered with your power
You were now but Napoleon Bonaparte
And should be so addressed.

NAPOLEON.

Well—Well—What more?

BERTRAND.

Sire, I blush to speak the rest.

NAPOLEON.

Go on—go on—

BERTRAND.

He then complained, my Liege, that you of late
Had kept your rooms so close his officers
Had been compelled to peep in through your windows
Or go without their due report of you.

NAPOLEON.

Well—Well—

BERTRAND.

I did not tell him of your illness, Sire—
Continuing he claimed :
That, now his government demanded,
He should communicate direct with you
Or through his own appointed methods ;
Ordered your doors should be kept open,
The blinds up from your windows, that he might
Have full assurance of your presence.

NAPOLEON.

Well—Well—You see I listen patiently—

BERTRAND.

That as before when you should walk or ride
His guards attend you.

NAPOLEON.

                How soon shall they enforce
These orders ?

BERTRAND.

            To-day, at four o' the clock,
Sir Hudson and his guards will wait on you—
'Tis close upon the hour.

NAPOLEON.

Summon our gentlemen
At once Bertrand—We will defend our honor
Or make a tragic end of it.

(Exit Bertrand.)

My sword, Marshand!

(Marshand presents sword.)

I will wear it—

(Marshand buckles the sword upon him.)

There seems a magic in its presence.
It is the insignia of authority.

(Marshand presents pistols.)

Ha? These are potent still! I can use these!
I was a good shot, Marshand, as you know—
I remember well my exploits at Brienne;
My comrades thought them wonderful.
I have killed birds flying in the air,
At thirty paces, with a weapon
Quite as small as this—Short range shall atone
Indifferent practice. Now on this meager rock
Shall we set up the last throne of Napoleon.
Drape our Imperial robe!

*(Marshand drapes the robe,
Napoleon regarding.)*

'Tis a prouder heritage than England's!

*(Re-enter Bertrand, attended by
Gen. Montholon, Gen. Gourgand,
M. De Las Casas and Dr.
O'Meara. All are armed. Bertrand conducts Napoleon to the im-
provised throne. His attendants
salute him.)*

Comrades: Short time have we for converse—
We are offered base humiliation,
Or a grave with heroes—I have chosen for you.

(They again salute him.)
*(Enter Sir Hudson Lowe,
officers and soldiers.)*

SIR HUDSON.

General Bonaparte—

BERTRAND.

(*Interrupting him.*)

Sir Hudson Lowe :
Communications for the Emperor
Should be addressed alone to Bertrand,
Grand Marshal of France.

SIR HUDSON.

What means this masquerade of royalty?
Throw down your arms ! Disperse !

NAPOLEON.

The Grand Marshal of France will thus reply
To St. Helena's Governor :
The Emperor holds not his titles
By the grace of England, but the accord
Of the enlightened world.   And say besides
That by the law of nations, civilized,
By custom even of barbaric tribes,
Who have the instinct of chivalric honor,
The terms of our embarkment on her ships
Made us the guest and not the prisoner
Of England.   The royal hospitality
That set apart for us this island rock
And clothed us with the dignity of "Subject,"
The high distinction of a British subject,
Vests us in rights, under the British rule,
Whereby our cottage is become our castle—
We shall defend it, to the extremity
Of honorable graves !

SIR HUDSON.

Are you so lost to reason as to lift
Your puny strength against the power of England?
You should not thus endanger the few days
Now left you—your grave is not far off.

NAPOLEON.

Through the long years of our captivity
Thou hast spared no effort thy low cunning
Could devise to annoy, to torture us!
I am ill—nigh unto death, mahap—
You come to taunt me, dying—Ah, my grave
Is not far off!—" Is not far off," saidst thou?
If so, beware the Nemesis!—
For I tell thee now, thou wart, grown putrid
On the hand of that Royal Infamy
That holds us prisoner here, even thou
Canst not escape! What though thou hast no soul?
Great Justice from my ashes shall invoke
A spirit will not leave out even thee
In its swift vengeance! 'Twill follow thee
And plague thee with such punishments as reach
The physical! Thou shalt crawl on through time,
Loathed as a leper, fœtid in disease—
Shunned as a pestilence, despised as filth,
A rotting reek, that spreads contagion;
Hated, as the assassin who in smiles
And tears and protestations of good faith
Administers slow poison! Thou art he—
The fittest wretch of all thy tribe—
Selected to command this prison rock!
Deceit, Intrigue and fawning Treachery
Have produced thee, Acme of Infamy!
Hell yawns for thee, not knowing yet
Thou art too base even for her vilest pool—
Begone! Ere that refuge is barred 'gainst thee!

(*Napoleon falls in Bertrand's arms
as Sir Hudson and suit go off
stage.*)

BERTRAND.

Ha! Ha! Ha! See how he sneaks away!
'Tis thus base reptiles steal out from the sun!

ACT VII.—SCENE SECOND.

PLANTATION HOUSE IN DISTANCE.

(Woodland)

(Enter Sir Hudson Lowe and officers.)

SIR HUDSON.

YOU have given the order ?

FIRST OFFICER.

I have.

SIR HUDSON.

Look, then, to its speedy execution !

FIRST OFFICER.

I will.

SIR HUDSON.

We'll transport all his hangers on, and see,
If then, he will remain so haughty. Come !

(Exeunt.)

*(Enter Napoleon, supported by
Marshand, attended by Gen. and
Mme. Bertrand, Gen. and Mme.
Montholon, Gen. Gourgaud, M.
De Las Casas and Dr. O'Meara.
English officers follow in the dis-
tance unobserved by Napoleon.)*

NAPOLEON.

When next from Homer you shall read to me,
Good Marshand, read of the funeral rites
Of noble Hector—
Bertrand, I shall meet Homer and converse with him?

BERTRAND.

Yes, Sire.

NAPOLEON.

    My Generals and friends
Shall join me ; Kleeber, Desaix, Lannes,
Massena, Besseires, Duroc, Ney,
And ye, the noble sharers of my exile !
Once more shall we experience the joy,
The intoxication of human glory !
We shall speak of what we have done and—and—
What we failed to do.

MONTHOLON.

    Think not upon that now, Sire !
Had we have been content—

NAPOLEON.

    Impossible !
A great soul may not be content !
There is no level for achieved pre-eminence
That may be endured by the truly great !
    I shall see Alexander
And Cæsar, and Hannibal and Frederick,
And Turenne and Conde ! We will converse
Of our profession—Unless in the upper spheres,
As here below, they shall object to seeing
A number of soldiers together.
        (*He discovers the English officers,*
        who have come forward and are

*listening, and turns upon them,
furiously.)*

Fall back, you wretched slaves ! Fall back, I say,
Or I will bid my valet whip you hence,
Impudent knaves !

(*They fall back.*)

MONTHOLON.

Patience ! Patience, my liege !
We are quite powerless now.

NAPOLEON.

Powerless
There is a halo 'round the truly great
As frightful to the eyes of craven souls
As all the thunderbolts of Jupiter !

(*Sinks in chair.*)

(*Recovering.*)
Is this Napoleon ? You see it was
My mind and not my body was of iron.
The sun is setting——
So hung the clouds, blood red, above that sun
When I to France did give my Josephine—
So hung they in the glare of burning Moscow—
So hung they o'er the field of Waterloo—
My fate's sad Trilogy !

(*Sinks.*)

(*Recovering.*)
The somber shadows sleep—
No wave of sound—My brain reels ! Is this death ?
  Ah ! Wondrous, incomparable pageantry !
What grand procession this of stately forms ?
The marshaled Glory of the Universe !
  All-wise, All-mighty, All-foreseeing Jove ;
Thou who in thunder-tones command'st the host
August, of the Immortals, hail ! All hail !

What holdest thou in keeping for the great?
    Silence!
Thou of the Silver-bow, Far-seeing
Phœbus Apollo; shall we be gods?
    Pallas Athene; answer me and tell
What life awaits beyond the tomb?
    Oh, Fate, my mother; Thou dost sit supreme
O'er all—Speak! Oh, speak!
            All, all is silence! 'Tis gone!—
What marvellous Perfection passeth now?
A crown of thorns—In His hands and feet and side
Are wounds—See! See who follows, worshipping!
Josephine!

                                        (*Sinks.*)

            (*Recovering and rising.*)
Charge, Ney, and yet the battle may be won!
Forward the Old Guard! Cry, France and victory!
They fall—they fall—they die! They cannot yield!
Forward the Old Guard! Forward! Forward!

———

Covers his face with his mantle and falls

DEAD.

GRAND TRANSFORMATION SCENE.

NAPOLEON,

WRAPPED IN HIS MILITARY CLOAK, ON THE ROCKY HEIGHTS OF
ST. HELENA, LOOKING OUT UPON THE SEA.

SPIRIT OF JOSEPHINE

HOVERING OVER, FLOATS DOWN UPON HIM.

THE EMBRACE IN ETERNITY.

THE END.

THE DYING NAPOLEON.

PREFATORY TO THE APPENDIX.

IN the appendix, herewith subjoined, will be found what, to my mind, is at once the most masterful, absolute argument in defence of the Divinity of Christ that has ever dropped from the lips of a man—the memorable words of Napoleon at St. Helena.

It was this immortal utterance that led me to an investigation of the life and character of the man, against whom the world has, for so long, spoken bitterly. I could not believe that the author of such sentiments could be the Napoleon of popular history.

It is in the hope that its reading may lead others to a search for the *facts*, and a consequent award of justice to the memory of Napoleon, that the appendix is offered.

R. S. DEMENT.

APPENDIX.

THE TESTIMONY OF NAPOLEON

TO THE

DIVINITY OF CHRIST

In a conversation with General Bertrand at St. Helena, Napoleon said :

"I know men, and I tell you that Jesus Christ is not a man. Superficial minds see a resemblance between Christ and the founders of empires, and the gods of other religions. That resemblance does not exist. There is between Christianity and whatever other religion the distance of infinity.

"We can say to the authors of every other religion, you are neither gods nor the agents of Deity. You are but missionaries of falsehood moulded from the same clay with the rest of mortals. You are made with all the passions and vices inseparable from them. Your temples and your priests proclaim your origin. Such will be the judgment, the cry of conscience of whoever examines the gods and the temples of paganism.

"Paganism was never accepted as truth by the wise men of Greece, neither by Socrates, Pythagoras, Plato, Anaxagoras, or Pericles. But, on the other side, the loftiest intellects since the advent of Christianity have had faith, a living faith, a practical faith in the mysteries and the doctrines of the Gospel; not only Bossuet and Fénelon, who were preachers, but Descartes and Newton, Leibnitz and Pascal, Corneille and Racine, Charlemagne and Louis XIV.

"Paganism is the work of man. One can here read but our imbecility. What do these gods, so boastful, know more than other mortals? These legislators, Greek or Roman? This Numa? This Lycurgus? These priests of India or of Memphis? This Confucius? This Mohammed? Absolutely nothing! There is not one among them all who has said anything new in reference to our future destiny, to the soul, to the essence of God, to the creation. Enter the sanctuaries of Paganism—you there find perfect chaos, a thousand contradictions, war between the gods, the immobility of sculpture, the division and rending of unity, the parceling out of the divine attributes, mutilated or denied in their essence, the sophisms of ignorance and presumption, polluted fetes, impurity and abomination adored, all sorts of corruption festering in the thick shades, with the rotten wood, the idol, and his priests. Does this honor God, or does it dishonor him? Are these religions and these gods to be compared with Christianity?

"As for me, I say no. I summon entire Olympus to my tribunal! I judge the gods, but am far from prostrating myself before their vain images. The gods, the legislators of India and of China, of Rome and of Athens, have nothing which can overawe me. Not that I am unjust to them; no, I appreciate them, because I know their value. Undeniably, princes whose existence is fixed in the memory as an image of order and of power, as the ideal of force and beauty, such princes were no ordinary men.

"I see in Lycurgus, Numa and Mohammed only legislators who, having the first rank in the state, have sought the best solution of the social problem; but I see nothing there which reveals divinity. They themselves have never raised their pretensions so high. As for me, I recognize the gods and these great men as beings like myself. They have performed a lofty part in their times, as I have done. Nothing announces them divine. On the contrary, there are numerous resemblances between them and myself, foibles and errors which ally them to me and to humanity.

"It is not so with Christ. Everything in Him astonishes me. Between Him and whoever else in the world, there is no possible term of comparison. He is truly a being of Himself. His ideas and His sentiments, the truths which He announces, His manner of convincing, are not explained either by human organization or by the nature of things.

"His birth, and the history of His life; the profundity of His doctrine, which grapples the mightiest difficulties, and which is, of those difficulties, the most admirable solution; His Gospel, His apparition, His empire, His march across the ages and the realms, everything, is for me a prodigy, a mystery insoluble, which plunges me into a reverie from which I can not escape, a mystery which is there before my eyes, a mystery which I can neither deny nor explain. Here I see nothing human.

"The nearer I approach, the more carefully I examine, everything is above me, everything remains grand—of a grandeur which overpowers. His religion is a revelation from an intelligence which certainly is not that of man. There is there a profound originality, which has created a series of words and maxims before unknown. Jesus borrowed nothing from our sciences. One can absolutely find nowhere, but in Him alone, the imitation or the example of His life. He is not a philosopher, since he advances by miracles, and, from the commencement, His disciples worshipped Him. He persuades them far more by an appeal to the heart than by any display of method and of logic. Neither did He impose upon them any preliminary studies or any knowledge of letters. All His religion consists in *believing*.

"In fact, the sciences and philosophy avail nothing for salvation; and Jesus came into the world to reveal the mysteries of heaven and the laws of the Spirit. Also, He has nothing to do but with the soul, and to that alone He brings His Gospel. The soul is sufficient for Him, as He is sufficient for the soul. Before Him the soul was nothing.

Matter and time were the masters of the world. At His voice everything returns to order. Science and philosophy become secondary. The soul has conquered its sovereignty. All the scholastic scaffolding falls, as an edifice ruined, before one single word—*faith*.

"What a master and what a word, which can effect such a revolution? With what authority does He teach men to pray? He imposes His belief, and no one, thus far, has been able to contradict Him ; first, because the Gospel contains the purest morality, and, also, because the doctrine which it contains, of obscurity, is only the proclamation and the truth of that which exists where no eye can see and no reason can penetrate. Who is the insensate who will say *no* to the intrepid voyager who recounts the marvels of the icy peaks which he alone has had the boldness to visit? Christ is that bold voyager. One can doubtless remain incredulous, but no one can venture to say *it is not so*.

"Moreover, consult the philosophers upon those mysterious questions which relate to the essence of man and to the essence of religion. What is their response? Where is the man of good sense who has ever learned anything from the system of metaphysics, ancient or modern, which is not truly a vain and pompous ideology, without any connection with our domestic life, with our passions? Unquestionably, with skill of thinking, one can seize the key of the philosophy of Socrates and Plato ; but, to do this, it is necessary to be a metaphysician ; and, moreover, with years of study, one must possess special aptitude. But good sense alone, the heart, an honest spirit, are sufficient to comprehend Christianity.

"The Christian religion is neither ideology nor metaphysics, but a practical rule which directs the actions of man, corrects him, counsels him, and assists him in all his conduct. The Bible contains a complete series of facts and of historical men, to explain time and eternity, such as no other religion has to offer. If this is not the true religion, one is very excusable in being deceived, for every thing in it is grand and worthy of God. I search in vain in history to find the similar to Jesus Christ, or anything which can approach the Gospel. Neither history, nor humanity, nor the ages, nor nature, can offer me anything with which I am able to compare it or explain it. Here everything is extraordinary. The more I consider the Gospel, the more I am assured that there is nothing there which is not beyond the march of events and above the human mind. Even the impious, themselves, have never dared to deny the sublimity of the Gospel, which inspires them with a sort of compulsory veneration. What happiness that Book procures for them who believe it! What marvels those admire there who reflect upon it. Book unique, where the mind finds a moral beauty before unknown, and an idea of the Supreme superior even to that which creation suggests! Who but God could produce that type, that ideal of perfection, equally exclusive and original?

"Christ, having but a few weak disciples, was condemned to death. He died the object of the wrath of the Jewish priests, and of the contempt of the nation, and abandoned and denied by His own disciples.

"'They are about to take me, and to crucify me,' said He. 'I shall be abandoned of all the world. My chief disciple will deny me at the commencement of my punishment. I shall be left to the wicked. But then, divine justice being satisfied, original sin being expiated by my sufferings, the bond of man to God will be renewed, and my death will be the life of my disciples. Then they will be more strong without me than with me, for they will see me rise again. I shall ascend to the skies, and I shall send them from heaven a spirit who will instruct them. The spirit of the cross will enable them to understand my Gospel. In fine, they will believe it, they will preach it and they will convert the world.'

"And this strange promise, so aptly called by Paul the

'foolishness of the cross;' this prediction of the miserably crucified, is literally accomplished, and the mode of the accomplishment is, perhaps, more prodigious than the promise.

"It is not a day nor a battle which has decided it. Is it the lifetime of a man? No! It is a war, a long combat of three hundred years, commenced by the apostles, and continued by their successors and by succeeding generations of Christians. In this conflict all the kings and all the forces of the earth were arrayed on one side. Upon the other I see no army, but a mysterious energy, individuals scattered here and there in all parts of the globe, having no other rallying sign than a common faith in the mysteries of the cross.

"What a mysterious symbol! The instrument of the punishment of the man-God. His disciples were armed with it. 'The Christ,' they said, 'God has died for the salvation of men.' What a strife, what a tempest these simple words have raised around the humble standard of the sufferings of the man-God! On the other side, we see rage and all the furies of hatred and violence ; on the other, there is gentleness, moral courage, infinite resignation. For three hundred years spirit struggled against brutality of sense, the conscience against the despotism, the soul against the body, virtue against all the vices. The blood of Christians flowed in torrents. They died kissing the hand which slew them. The soul alone protested, while the body surrendered itself to all tortures. Everywhere Christians fell, and everywhere they triumphed.

"You speak of Cæsar, of Alexander; of their conquests, and of the enthusiasm they enkindled in the hearts of their soldiers ; but can you conceive of a dead man making conquests with an army faithful and entirely devoted to his memory? My armies have forgotten me, even while living, as the Carthaginian army forgot Hannibal. Such is our power! A single battle lost crushes us, and adversity scatters our friends.

"Can you conceive of Cæsar, the eternal emperor of the Roman senate, and from the depths of his mausoleum governing the empire, watching over the destinies of Rome? Such is the history of the invasion and conquest of the world by Christianity. Such is the power of the God of the Christians; and such is the perpetual miracle of the progress of the faith and of the government of His Church. Nations pass away, thrones crumble, but the Church remains. What is, then, the power that has protected this Church, thus assailed by the furious billows of rage and the hostility of ages? Where is the arm which, for eighteen hundred years, has protected the Church from so many storms which have threatened to engulf it?

"In every other existence, but that of Christ, how many imperfections! Where is the character which has not yielded vanquished by obstacles? Where is the individual who has never been governed by circumstances or places, who has never succumbed to the influence of the times, who has never compined with any customs or passions? From the first day to the last, He is the same, always the same, majestic and simple, infinitely firm and infinitely gentle.

"Truth should embrace the universe. Such is Christianity, the only religion which destroys sectional prejudice, the only one which proclaims the unity and the absolute brotherhood of the whole human family, the only one which is purely spiritual—in fine, the only one which assigns to all, without distinction, for a true country the bosom of the Creator, God. Christ proved that He was the son of the Eternal by His disregard of *time*. All His doctrines signify one only and the same thing—*Eternity*.

"It is true that Christ proposed to our faith a series of mysteries. He commands, with authority, that we should believe them, giving no other reason than those tremendous words, 'I *am* God.' He declares it. What an abyss He creates by that declaration between Himself and all the fabricators of religion! What audacity, what sacrilege, what blasphemy, if it were not true! I say more; the universal triumph of an affirmation of that kind, if the triumph were not really that of God himself, would be a plausible excuse and a reason for atheism.

"Moreover, in propounding mysteries, Christ is harmonious with Nature, which is profoundly mysterious. From whence do I come? Whither do I go? Who am I? Human life is a mystery in its origin, its organization, and its end. In man and out of man, in nature, everything is mysterious. And can one wish that religion should not be mysterious? The creation and the destiny of the world are an unfathomable abyss, as also is the creation and the destiny of each individual. Christianity, at least, does not evade these great questions. It meets them boldly. And our doctrines are a solution of them for every one who believes.

The Gospel possesses a secret virtue, a mysterious efficacy, a warmth which penetrates and soothes the heart. One finds in meditating upon it that which one experiences in contemplating the heavens. The Gospel is not a book; it is a living being, with an action, a power which invades everything that opposes its extension. Behold it upon this table, this Book surpassing all others" (here the Emperor solemnly placed his hand upon it); "I never omit to read it, and every day with the same pleasure.

"Nowhere is to be found such a series of beautiful ideas, admirable moral maxims, which defile, like the battalions of a celestial army, and which produce in our soul the same emotion which one experiences in contemplating the infinite expanse of the skies, resplendent on a summer's night with all the brilliance of the stars. Not only is our mind absorbed, it is controlled, and the soul can never go astray with this Book for its guide. Once master of our spirit, the faithful Gospel loves us. God, even, is our friend, our father, and truly our God. The mother has no greater care for the infant whom she nurses.

"What a proof of the divinity of Christ! With an empire

so absolute, He has but one single end, the spiritual melior-
ation of individuals, the purity of conscience, the union to
that which is true, the holiness of the soul.

"Christ speaks, and at once generations become His by
stricter, closer ties than those of blood—by the most sacred,
the most indissoluble of all unions. He lights up the flame
of a love which consumes self-love, which prevails over every other love. The founders of other religions never conceived of this mystical love, which is the essence of Christianity, and is beautifully called charity. In every attempt
to effect this thing, namely, *to make himself beloved*, man
deeply feels his own impotence. So that Christ's greatest
miracle undoubtedly is the reign of charity.

"I have so inspired multitudes that they would die for
me. God forbid that I should form any comparison between the enthusiasm of the soldier and Christian charity,
which are as unlike as their cause. But, after all, my presence was unnecessary; the lightning of my eye, my voice,
a word from me, then the sacred fire was kindled in their
hearts. I do, indeed, possess the secret of this magical power, which lifts the soul, but I could never impart it to any
one. None of my generals ever learned it from me; nor
have I the means of perpetuating my name, and love for me,
in the hearts of men, and to effect these things without physical means.

"Now that I am at St. Helena, now that I am alone,
chained upon this rock, who fights and wins empires for
me? Who are the courtiers of my misfortune? Who thinks
of me? Who makes efforts for me in Europe? Where are my
friends? Yes, two or three, whom your fidelity immortal-
izes, you share, you console my exile."

(Here the voice of the Emperor trembled with emotion,
and for a moment he was silent. He then continued:

"Yes, our life once shone with all the brilliance of the
diadem and the throne; and yours, Bertrand, reflected that
splendor, as the dome of the Invalides, gilt by us, reflects

the rays of the sun. But disasters came ; the gold gradual-
ly became dim. The ruin of misfortune and outrage with
which I am daily deluged has effaced all the brightness. We
are mere lead now, General Bertrand, and soon I shall be in
my grave.

"Such is the fate of great men ! So it was with Cæsar
and Alexander. And I, too, am forgotten. And the name
of a conqueror and an emperor is a college theme ! Our exploits are tasks given to pupils by their tutor, who sit in
judgment upon us, awarding censure or praise. And mark
what is soon to become of me ! Assassinated by the English
oligarchy, I die before my time ; and my dead body, too,
must return to the earth, to become food for the worms.
Behold the destiny near at hand, of him who has been called
the great Napoleon ! What an abyss between my deep misery and the eternal reign of Christ, which is proclaimed,
loved, adored, and which is extending all over the earth !
Is this to die? Is it not rather to live? The death of
Christ ! It is the death of God.

"General Bertrand, if you do not perceive that Jesus
Christ is God, very well, then I did wrong to make you a
general."

www.ingramcontent.com/pod-product-compliance
Lightning Source LLC
Chambersburg PA
CBHW031113020726
47495CB00007B/2176